LARKSPUR DREAMS

This Large Print Book carries the
Seal of Approval of N.A.V.H.

LARKSPUR DREAMS

ANITA HIGMAN AND JANICE A. THOMPSON

THORNDIKE PRESS

A part of Gale, Cengage Learning

GALE
CENGAGE Learning

Detroit • New York • San Francisco • New Haven, Conn • Waterville, Maine • London

GALE
CENGAGE Learning™

Thorndike Press® Large Print Christian Romance.
The text of this Large Print edition is unabridged.
Other aspects of the book may vary from the original edition.
Set in 16 pt. Plantin.

LIBRARY OF CONGRESS CATALOGING-IN-PUBLICATION DATA

Higman, Anita.
  Larkspur dreams / by Anita Higman & Janice Thompson. —
Large print ed.
    p. cm. — (Ozark weddings; bk. 1) (Thorndike Press large
print Christian romance)
  ISBN-13: 978-1-4104-3850-8
  ISBN-10: 1-4104-3850-3
    1. Weddings—Fiction. 2. Large type books. I. Thompson,
Janice A. II. Title.
PS3558.I374L37 2011
813'.54—dc22
                                                            2011012365

Published in 2011 by arrangement with Barbour Publishing, Inc.

Printed in the United States of America
1 2 3 4 5 6 7 15 14 13 12 11

To three amazing women . . . Kim Watson, Kristen Lawrence, and Sylvia Thompson. What treasures you are to this world.

Much gratitude goes to my daughter, Hillary Higman, for her honest input and support.

Thanks goes to Val Vogt for helping me understand the life of an artist.

Anita Higman

To all of the "Larkspurs" in my life. You know who you are. Your creative spirits uplift, encourage, and bring a smile to this face when I need it most.

Janice A. Thompson

ONE

What a scene! Lark sat in her Hummer. The move-in day of her rich neighbor certainly had a sitcom quality to it. She leaned in to watch him. Mr. New Guy gestured to the movers about his leather furniture, but they held to their standard *modus operandi* — the heave-ho method. And Lark could tell her dear, old friend, Skelly Piper, had the new guy cornered with his zucchini brownies and the highlights of his hernia operation.

Is that truly a pair of boxers flying up in the breeze? Apparently they had blown out from an open carton and were doubling as a kite. The offending object finally landed in a tree and began flapping like a white flag. *So how does a guy look manly while retrieving unmentionables from a blue spruce?*

Just as Lark was about to find out, her eyes followed a new addition to the bedlam. *Oh, no. Not Picasso!* Her pet duck had yet to be approved by the planning commission, and he was waddling about on her new neighbor's walkway being loose in more than one sense of the word.

I'd better go help Mr. New Guy out. She rolled the window down and let her Christian rock music soar free into the air. With her brightest smile, she waved to her new neighbor. Skelly Piper saluted back, but Mr. New Guy sported a croaking sort of smirk that seemed to be directed at her.

Lark cut the engine and strode over to the two men. "Hi." She hugged Skelly as he said his good-byes.

"Oh, and see ya at the fall festival, kiddo." Skelly shuffled off, bowlegged. His thick hair stuck up on his head like a clump of silver grass. But he had his usual warm smile as he glanced back at her.

Turning to her new neighbor, Lark couldn't help but notice God had been quite charitable with his appearance. He had a striking presence with his hazel eyes, short brown locks, and a "surely he must lift weights" kind of build. *Hmm. Early to mid-thirties, same as me. Same medium height. But who wears a suit to move in?* And his tie looked like it would work equally well as a tourniquet. Lark also took note that Mr. New Guy held the bow on the sack of brownies as if he were holding the tail of a dead skunk.

Lark extended her hand to welcome him. "I'm Larkspur Wendell, your next-door neighbor."

"I'm Everett Holden III," he said like a maitre d' with an attitude. He slipped his Palm Pilot into his suit pocket and shook her hand.

The word *mannequin* popped into Lark's head, but his fingers and gaze lingered a moment longer than she expected.

One of the movers sneezed loudly, and all at once the assessing moment dissipated. They quickly freed each other's hand.

Everett looked down at his ultra-polished wingtips.

Lark wondered if he could use them for rearview mirrors. Picasso toddled over to her. "And who let you out?" She shook her finger at the duck as he dipped his head in shame.

"You actually *own* that flying outhouse?" Everett asked without a speck of humor.

"I'm sorry he left a bunch of his . . . doodling artistry all over your walkway. But you know, he doesn't usually get out. Perhaps someone *let* him out."

Everett straightened his already immovable posture. "Well, *I* certainly didn't do it."

9

A belch reverberated out of one of the movers. She tucked her giggle away, folded her arms, and nodded in the direction of the two guys lugging a couch up the steep steps to the house. "I rest my case."

"Okay," Everett said. "Mutt and Jeff over there might have accidentally done it since our gates are next to each other, but generally you *do* keep that thing penned up, right?" His brows furrowed a bit.

"I assure you, Picasso's not been trained as an attack duck." Lark could barely hold back her mirth. She took a treat out of her pants pocket and tossed it to Picasso. He rewarded her with a few happy mutterings.

"So do you run a game preserve back there?" Everett asked.

"No. Just one sweet, little mallard that thinks I'm his momma." His face grasped her attention. "And what do you do, Mr. Everett Holden III?" *I can't wait to see what this amazingly uptight guy is going to say next.*

Everett smiled as if it were a new expression he was trying out. "I'm an accountant, and I'm going to work out of my home. I spend most of the day behind the computer, but it suits me. I like quiet. Well, actually, I require it." He raised his head and made a little sniffing noise.

Lark tried to smooth the folds of her

angora sweater. She gave up and looked over at Everett's gingerbread cottage. She couldn't imagine him buying such a dainty, rosy-colored house. "You certainly bought a pretty place to live."

He glanced at his home and then nodded. "It should be an excellent investment."

Lark waited for him to say more, but he just stared at his house. Many homes in the neighborhood were Victorian with pocket gardens, but she also loved the charm of the whole town with its galleries, trolleys, and quaint shops. For now, though, she couldn't help wondering if her new neighbor had also been captivated by the delight of Eureka Springs.

Everett tapped his shoe against a rock.

Okay, it's time for me to leave. "I've kept you too long. I'm so sorry." She turned to go. "By the way, we all have get-togethers around the holidays."

"Holidays?"

Surely Everett hadn't forgotten Thanksgiving would be arriving in just a few weeks. "You know, Thanksgiving and Christmas?" Lark said.

Everett shifted his weight as if he were losing patience. "I realize *what* holidays. I'm just not used to spending them with anyone."

Lark could feel her mouth gape open. What could she possibly say in response to that? She looked back at Everett. "Oh, but to spend Christmas alone sounds so . . . I mean . . . wouldn't it be lonesome?"

"I don't know. I've not spent a lot of time thinking about it." Everett straightened the sleeve of his suit, making Picasso think he had a treat. As her duck waddled toward his shoes, Everett took a conspicuous step away.

"I always have guests over around Thanksgiving, so I hope you'll be one of them."

Everett looked up at the sky as if he were expecting bad weather. "I really hate to obligate myself right away. But thank you."

What a peculiar response. "You're welcome," Lark said. "By the way, you'll enjoy your new neighbors. They're down-to-earth, generous, and practically like family."

"That's nice. By the way, do you mind?" Everett pointed at Picasso's handiwork. "You know, hosing that off my walkway?"

Lark jolted back from her reverie. "Oh, yes. I'll clean it up."

Everett nodded.

"I'll say bye for now," Lark said.

"Good-bye."

Lark turned to leave, but when she heard the pounding of piano keys, she glanced back. The movers lifted an old, high back piano down from the truck. "Do you play?"

"Excuse me?" Everett asked.

Lark motioned toward the instrument. "The piano. Do you play?"

"No. I don't." His frosty countenance softened, giving him a boy-like appearance. "It was my mother's."

"Well, it's a pity. With some lessons I'll bet you could make it come to life."

"I don't think I have enough aptitude."

"All you need is the passion. Then everything else falls into place . . . like colors on a canvas." She wondered if the piano made him nostalgic. She could tell he had a smile aching to be released. A good sign. It meant Everett had a warm, beating heart under his cool, starched veneer, and a handsome man with heart would make good cocoa-sharing company on a cold evening.

Lark wiggled her fingers in a wave and headed toward her backyard gate, which she could see had indeed been left ajar. Without any commands, Picasso followed Lark. She sang to him softly as he waddled next to her along the limestone path. Before shutting the latch, Lark glanced toward Everett. He'd been caught gazing at her. Why did his interest give her so much pleasure?

Quickly Everett turned away and headed toward the delights of Mutt and Jeff.

13

"Well, what do you think of our new neighbor?" she whispered to her duck. "I think he reminds me of my old university professor, Dr. Norton." Picasso paused to look up at her and then toddled on his way with his tail feathers wagging. Lark recalled her professor had craved such a private life he eventually left his career. In fact, he'd become so withdrawn, one by one everyone left him to his lonely existence. "We'll watch out for our new neighbor, won't we, little fellow?" Picasso continued to have nothing to say on the subject, so she secured him in his large habitat and blew a kiss in his direction.

A gust of crisp, autumn air turned Lark's mind to the church's fall festival. She wished she'd remembered to invite Everett. She could tell he needed to get out. *Maybe I can ask him later.*

Lark scooted into her old tire swing and gazed up at the cornflower blue heavens. *Such a nice color, God.* She shoved off toward the sky.

Just as Lark wrapped up her prayer, she realized she'd reached the highest point she'd ever gone in her swing. She felt suspended in midair like a cloud. As if the day had stopped just for her to enjoy a moment longer. Lark slowed her speed and then locked her arms to let her body drift low. She'd always loved swinging that way when she was growing up. Her parents did, too. Right alongside her.

Lark stopped her swinging and shook her head. She pondered how one thoughtless act of an intoxicated driver could affect her life so deeply. Sending her mom and dad to heaven early. She sighed. *I miss you both so much.*

Lark refused to dwell on the parts of her life she couldn't control, so she released her sorrow as she took in a deep breath. The late October air smelled of earth and foliage and wood smoke. Mmm. Her favorite time of the year in Arkansas. And so magnificent with the autumn leaves setting the hills ablaze with gold and orange and crimson.

She picked up an acorn from her little pile and then released it again. The nut struck the mound and then rolled off in an unexpected direction, making the whole stack of acorns scatter, as well.

Lark thought having a brand-new neighbor was like her tiny acorn drama. She wondered how God would allow Everett Holden to change her life. Neighbors always did. At least, *Lark's* neighbors always did. Or did she change *their* lives? She wasn't sure in the end who influenced whom more.

It appeared all of humanity bounced off each other, with each movement and word affecting the whole like a loose nut pouncing on a mound of acorns. Whether acorns or humans, the conclusion remained the same. Life was pure adventure. One never knew for sure what would happen next.

Two

Everett handed the movers a check and shut the door to his one-hundred-year-old house. *Ahh. Quiet at last.* He looked at the stone fireplace and polished wooden floors. In spite of the ornate qualities of the exterior, the home suited him well, and he liked the idea of moving to a quiet, woodsy village amidst the Ozark Mountains. Best of all was the convenience factor, since his biggest client lived in Eureka Springs.

After making some serious money as an accountant, Everett looked forward to reaping the benefits. But he wasn't about to lose what he'd gained, so that meant no distractions. Living in a smaller community would help. His Realtor had promised him that in spite of all the tourists, the neighborhood was so quiet, one could hear a pin drop. *Perfect.*

Except for that woman next door. Larkspur Wendell certainly could be a potential distraction. *And attractive enough to cause a traffic pileup.* What was it with those brown eyes of hers anyway? She had a probing gaze, which made one wonder if she knew everyone's shadowy secrets and fully intended to use them. Yes, there was mischief written all over her lovely face. If he ever planned to get any work done, passive resistance and neutrality would need to be his watchwords when it came to Lark. He almost chuckled, but instead walked over to the piano and closed the lid.

Everett heard the doorbell and thought it might be the movers coming back to give his furniture one more bash with their crowbar, but a quick peek told him it was his neighborly distraction instead. He opened the door with his passive resistance intact. To his surprise Lark stood before him dressed in a bee costume. "May I help you?"

Lark smiled as one of her shoulders came toward her cheek in a shy kind of shrug. Was that her perfume drifting over to him?

Everett loosened his tie a bit.

"Hi. I know you're unpacking and all."

Good calculation.

Lark reached up to adjust one of the antennas on her head. "But our church is having a fall festival later this evening. And I wanted to invite you."

"It's hard to take you seriously. You're dressed . . . like an insect." He held back a chuckle.

"Tell me, Mr. Holden. What do you *really* see?"

What does she mean? "I see a lady dressed like an insect."

A warm smile inched its way across Lark's face. Her hair floated around her in the breeze as she wiped the strands from her eyes. "Well, you also see a neighbor who wants you to feel welcome."

"Okay." It was a struggle for him to drum up any animosity since Lark seemed so sincere.

"I give away candy and run the win-a-goldfish game," she said. "That's why I have on this costume. I have to be there early to get set up, but here's the address if you decide to come. We'll also have a cakewalk, a white elephant sale, and plenty of hot dogs." She offered him a folded piece of paper along with a packet of chewing gum.

Everett accepted both items, but he wasn't going to bother asking why she was dressed like a bee instead of a goldfish. He figured her answer would be as tangible as her gauzy wings.

"You're certainly —"

"Listen." Was that one of his headaches

coming on? "I *will* be looking for a church in this neighborhood, but right now I've got to get my office set up and get back to work. Maybe some other time." *Do I really mean that?* He'd been a Christian since childhood, but sometimes he had to admit his church attendance had taken a backseat to his work.

"No problem. But don't work too hard. If you're not careful, Mr. Holden, you'll miss the *joie de vivre.*" Lark whirled around, just missing his face with her wings. Oblivious to her near hit, she headed down the walk humming something he'd heard in Sunday school when he was a kid, "Go Tell It on the Mountain."

Everett watched her go as he placed his hand on his arm where she'd touched him. *What did she mean?* He'd miss the *joie de vivre?*

Before he closed the door, he noticed a man sporting a bomber jacket and a ponytail rumble up to Larkspur's house on a motorcycle. He looked like something off a billboard promoting filterless cigarettes and a tattooed lifestyle. Why did some people generate noise just by existing? The thunder from his bike echoed through the canyons. *Who does he remind me of anyway? Oh yeah. My brother, Marty.* He hadn't heard from him in years and suddenly wondered what had become of him.

The revving of the engine forced him to refocus his attention on Lark. She slipped on her suede jacket and hopped onto the back of the guy's bike as if she'd done it many times. *Must be her boyfriend.* He told himself that when he did have the time to date again, it would be with a woman who had her feet firmly planted on the earth's surface.

Everett put a stick of the gum in his mouth before he remembered he hated candy. Hmm. He hadn't chewed licorice gum since he was a kid. Kind of an odd, sweet flavor. He stuck the packet in his shirt pocket and headed to the stacks of boxes in his office. But the second he hit the office door, he knew what he would do next. He'd look up the meaning of *joie de vivre* in his French-English dictionary.

After the festival, Lark removed her coat and bee wings. She smiled, remembering how the faces of the children lit up when they'd won a goldfish. *And I still can't believe The Salt and Light Band played all my favorite songs.* She'd also been pleased to see so many new people in the crowd. And some were interested in checking out the church on Sunday morning. *What a success.* She sank into the couch, exhausted but content.

Lark closed her eyes for a moment and thought of Everett. At the festival she'd glanced around looking for him, but she knew he had the perfect excuse for not attending. He was still busy unpacking. *I wonder if he'll ever become a part of the community.* She certainly couldn't imagine him wanting to spend the holidays all alone.

Lark thought of Dr. Norton again and pulled down one of her yearbooks from the university. She flipped the pages back and forth until she found her professor's photo. She studied the picture. So forlorn with a hint of something else. Desperation? She touched his photo. Rumor was, he'd not only lost his wife and friends because of his reclusive lifestyle, but he'd also died a lonely death. Only three people had come to his funeral, including herself. Strange, he'd willingly chosen his solitary way of life. Lark wondered what trauma in Dr. Norton's past had made him so self-destructive.

But there was still hope for Everett. She vowed to rally round her neighbor. Whatever it took, she'd help him out of his solitary existence.

THREE

Everett woke up feeling as animated as dirt. During the night he'd conjured up his usual array of nightmares.

Is that the doorbell? He realized the constant *ding-dong*ing had awakened him. He rarely slept in, but he'd stayed up late clearing out boxes. By the time he'd finished, he dropped from exhaustion. No time to grumble. He'd see to the door, get rid of whoever it was, and then get busy finishing up his office.

Everett stumbled over a shoe, nearly smacking his head on a bedpost. His brain whispered the word *caffeine.* And lots of it. *No time right now,* he told himself as he yanked on a pair of old jeans and a T-shirt. He made his way to the front door, but just as he opened it, a Pets Lovers of America van sped away from the curb leaving a trail of blue smoke. There on his porch sat a large cage. A parrot, the colors of a Hawaiian shirt, sat perched on a twig. Everett leaned down to the level of the bird's eye. "Who are you?"

The animal scooted across the branch and crooked his neck upward as if to size him up. "Who are you?" the parrot repeated.

Great. A yapping parrot. Was it a delivery gone awry? Well, maybe the feathery varmint really belonged to Larkspur, the lady with the duck. And if not, maybe she'd at least want to take it off his hands.

The last thing on his agenda, though, was to get entangled in Lark's day. His head began to throb. He threw on a coat, picked up the parrot, and headed next door.

Everett's attention turned toward the street. Okay, so why was there a Fayetteville television van parked in front of Lark's home? How could he have missed seeing the vehicle before? Everett marched to Lark's house, bypassed the bell, and hammered on her door with his fist.

A man with a goatee and a notebook opened the door. "Lark does have a doorbell. You must be Everett from next door. I see you brought Igor."

Who is this guy? "I'm afraid I don't understand any of this —"

"I'm afraid," the parrot repeated with a noisy mocking sound.

The man with the wimpy beard laughed. "Well, both of you come on in. Lark's in her loft. We just finished the interview up there. We wanted to be where she creates."

"Creates what?" He set the parrot down and glanced around inside. Sunlight poured in through the large windows. Immense paintings hung on every wall. Countryside scenes were filled with people caught up in everyday life.

Everett gazed at a painting of a girl wearing a sun hat and playing with a lamb. The word *realism* came to mind from a required art class in college. Even though the picture depicted life a hundred years ago, it looked welcoming and real enough to make him want to step into the landscape. And he also caught the unmistakable influence of the Ozarks in her work. *Fascinating.*

Then he remembered what Lark had said about *joie de vivre.* In French it meant the "sweetness of life." Those words seemed to describe the painting completely. He felt himself falling into some kind of emotional black hole. *Back to reality.*

The goatee guy headed up the metal, spiral staircase. *She must have done some remodeling on this old house.* Everett heard laughter upstairs, so out of curiosity, he picked up the cage and followed the man.

"You mean you didn't even know your neighbor was Larkspur Wendell, the illustrator?"

Everett felt annoyed with his cheeky attitude. "Illustrator of what?"

The goatee guy stopped midway and turned around just to frown at him. "You know — *When Dragons Fly, In a Giddy Pickle,* or the *Electric Seeds* series?" The guy looked at him as if *he* were the creature in a cage.

Everett shook his head but wanted to pelt the guy with birdseed. *I should have had my coffee.*

The goatee guy shrugged his shoulders and continued up the stairs. "I tell you, she's one of a kind. I just love Lark."

Before either of them could say another word, they arrived at the top of the stairs. The French doors were open, and Everett could see Lark sitting on a stool at an art table. Her long, dark hair flowed around her slender shoulders. Even in overalls, she was no doubt a beauty, but even more than that, Lark had a distinct presence in the room. He could barely remember why he was so irritated.

Lark didn't see him as the two men stepped into the room. A female reporter chatted with her while some guy packed up his camera.

Lark turned around to him. Everett noticed the radiance in her eyes, akin to the sun coming up in the morning.

She jumped up and hugged him.

Everett brought his free hand up on her back for a pat.

"I just love Lark," the parrot repeated and then squawked.

Everyone burst into laughter except Everett.

"I'm so glad you're here. You brought Igor. By the way, he likes to repeat things." Lark wiggled her eyebrows. "So be careful what you say."

Everett frowned. "Well, I didn't. I mean —"

Lark looked at him as if they'd always been friends. "He's your housewarming gift. I had him delivered from Springdale. I thought since you were all alone, Igor could keep you company."

FOUR

A cough erupted from Everett's mouth. Just as he was about to explain himself, the female reporter lifted her chin as if to bring the conversation back to business.

"We have everything we need," the reporter said. "Thanks for your time, Ms. Wendell. You were marvelous." She lifted the lapel mike off Lark's overalls and shook her hand. "By the way, if I leave without an autograph for my daughter, I'll be in trouble tonight."

Lark gave each crew member a hand-signed piece of art and a hug good-bye. She stayed in the room with him, while the crew filed down the staircase. To avoid the Igor topic, he found himself simply glancing around, taking in the various aspects of the room. Light purple walls with a sign over the door that read, "IMAGINE." Flower petals strewn on the floor. Electric guitar on a stand in the corner. Books and art magazines stacked here and there and a bowl full of jellybeans on the floor near a beanbag chair. "Aren't you going downstairs to lock your door?"

"No. We have very little crime here. In fact, sometimes I forget to lock up."

This woman is so naive. "You're being a bit . . . reckless," Everett said. "Don't you think?"

Lark walked over to the birdcage. "You don't like Igor, do you?"

Everett switched gears. "Why did you *really* buy me a talking parrot? You could have just brought me brownies. I like brownies." *Well, until I tasted Skelly's.*

"Why *not* buy a talking parrot?" Lark looked at Igor and smiled. "I saw him online, and he seemed like a gift you might enjoy. I really —"

"But how would you know that?" Everett rubbed his aching head. "You don't even know me. And I know it must have been very expensive."

"Don't you like pets?"

Everett shifted his weight. Keeping up with his neighbor's conversation was as exasperating as using a cup to empty a sinking boat. "Let's just say, pets don't agree with me."

Lark laughed. A bubbling kind of giggle

that wasn't an altogether unpleasant sound.

"They don't agree with you?" Lark asked. "It's not like you're going to eat Igor for dinner."

"Igor for dinner." The bird shrieked and ruffled his feathers.

"I appreciate the thought, but I have no time for pets. I work long hours. He would be neglected, so I'd like *you* to have . . . Igor." Everett saw a little light go out of Lark's eyes. Something made him want to bring that light back, but he wasn't sure why. He might have to think on that one later. "I mean, it would be like turning my house into a resort for flying animals." *Guess I shouldn't have said that last part. Why is she staring at my clothes?* He looked down at his jeans, which were full of holes. And his feet were bare. *Not good.* He wondered how that happened. He never did that sort of thing. Well, at least the cold front hadn't made it through yet.

Lark opened the cage door. "Hi there, Igor. You're a sweetie."

"You're a sweetie," the bird said back to her.

Lark chuckled as she stroked his neck. The bird dipped his head next to her hand and closed its eyes.

While Lark appeared distracted, Everett

took note that her office had no blinds or curtains at the huge window. Most people put up drapes and heavy shutters, but as an artist she must like to use the natural light.

He stepped over to her art table and looked at one of her watercolor paintings. The sheet of rough, white paper seemed to come to life with rabbits, foxes, and turtles all hiding among the ferns and tree trunks. The fanciful pictures were no less than what? Enchanting? He'd better not get caught using *that* word in public.

But the illustrations reminded him of an earlier time in his life when he used to read to children at one of the local hospitals in Fayetteville. Amazing. He used to actually volunteer his time, and he'd loved it. But that seemed like a lifetime ago, before life had taught him the lessons of unspeakable misfortune. "You didn't mention you were an artist."

"Well, you were busy herding your movers," Lark said. "And it seemed like they needed a little *coaching* as I recall."

She had more paint on her lavender overalls than on her paper. He saw her eyes searching his again. But what could she be looking for? "This current work here — is it to illustrate a new book?"

"No, I did it just for fun." Lark smiled

31

down at the painting. "The idea came from a dream I had. So I thought I'd try to capture it."

"So you have pleasant dreams?" Everett asked.

"Almost always. Do you?"

He almost said no but then admonished himself for nearly sharing intimate details about his life. "It's rather hard to explain." Maybe he just needed to get back to work.

"I'm sorry about the gift," Lark said. "Sometimes I've been known to be a little too — spur-of-the-moment. It's one of my great weaknesses. But I assure you, God and I are working on it."

"Apology accepted." He offered her a wide smile since he was glad to be rid of Igor, but he wondered just how "spur-of-the-moment" she was and how many "weaknesses" she and God were working on. Suddenly he heard a series of clatters and bangs. "What's that racket?"

"Oh, it's Skelly. Our neighbor. He sometimes throws pots and pans at his brick wall."

"How peculiar. Why does he do that?" Everett wanted to see what was happening, but he knew Skelly's backyard wasn't visible from her window.

Lark stroked her hands along her arms.

"Skelly lost his wife to cancer a few months ago. You know, when her hair fell out from the treatments, she wore a baseball cap. And wherever they went, Skelly always wore a baseball cap, too. Just so she wouldn't feel different or alone. Rose is in heaven now." Lark smiled at him with a faraway gaze. "I loved the way they loved each other." She shrugged. "So now he bakes everyone brownies just like his wife did, he prays a lot, and sometimes, when he misses her terribly, he finds it helpful to throw a few pots and pans against his brick wall. Why not, if it helps?"

"I'm sorry for Skelly. That must be hard." Everett paused, not really knowing how to respond to the man's sorrow, so he decided to change the subject. "But I still think you should lock your doors. I saw a hooligan-type last evening."

"Really?" Lark tied her long hair back with a clip and took a step closer to him.

"Yes. That riffraff on the bike. You know, the one who offered the *bee* a ride with no helmets." He raised an eyebrow and then rebuked himself for judging someone he barely knew.

Lark looked surprised. "That *riffraff,* who was kind enough to drive me to the church fall festival yesterday, happens to be Jeremy, our youth pastor."

Everett swallowed hard, but he felt like another retaliating remark building up. "Well, I hope he doesn't have a wife."

"Jeremy is single, and we go out from time to time. *And,* I might add, he's got a very successful teen ministry. Now don't you feel a little . . . silly?"

"I've never been *silly* in my life," Everett said.

"I'll bet you haven't, Mr. Holden." Her lips curled up at the edges.

"I'll bet you haven't," the bird squawked back at them.

"Oh, shut up," Everett said. *Oh man. Now I'm talking to animals. Time to go.* Everett looked away from Lark's bemused expression to stare out her workroom window. He noticed her office window was directly facing his own large office window. And the windows were only a few feet apart. A groan welled up inside him. "If you'll excuse me, I still have twenty-one boxes to unpack." He turned and moved toward the stairs.

Moments later, Everett offered his goodbye at the door. He knew the words came off rather strangled, but he felt more determined than ever to keep Lark at a safe distance. And he wasn't about to make this community his new family as Lark suggested. He repeated his mantra. "Passive resistance and neutrality."

What was it about this guy? Exasperating. Lonely. But so cute. Or maybe one of the things that captured her interest was his expression of subtle yearning.

She plunked down on her love seat, pulled a sprig of baby's breath from the vase, and stroked the tiny blossoms across her cheek. Lark suddenly thought of Jeremy. So dedicated and funny and genuine. In fact, he had so many good and godly qualities about him, she'd be crazy not to think of him in more serious terms. But she'd known since girlhood Mr. Lifetime would be poles apart from her. Like south meeting north and then trying to find a common parallel. She knew in her heart the Christian man she'd marry someday would not only garner her admiration and affection . . . but also leave her breathless.

She rested her feet on the coffee table. *Yes, an acorn has fallen,* Lark thought. *And Everett's neatly stacked pile is about to be scattered.*

FIVE

Lark stretched her arms out to a new morning. Sunday had gone well. Church had been good, but now Monday morning beckoned. The clock on the night table read 6:30 a.m. She never bothered with setting her alarm but instead let her natural body rhythms tell her when she'd had enough sleep. She flipped the light on and smiled at the bird in his cage. "Good morning, Igor."

Bits of his softness floated about the cage as he fluffed his feathers. "Good morning, Igor," the bird repeated.

Lark shoved her lavender comforter back, slid her wiggling toes into her slippers, and got up. She chatted softly to Igor as she checked his food and water supply. Still wearing her long, granny nightshirt, she padded up the spiral staircase, letting her hand slide along the cool metal railing up to her loft. No need for coffee since she let music rev her creative juices in the morning. Once in her studio, she flipped on her lights and her amplifier, strapped on her guitar, and prepared to rock. Was that classical music she heard coming from Everett's office? *Seems kind of loud.* She listened closely. *Wow! Vivaldi. Wind and brass. Cool.*

She didn't see Everett standing anywhere in his office so she decided to enhance the music with her own hard rock. *Oh yeah. Oboe Concerto in D Minor.* Lark positioned her fingers on the neck of the guitar and tapped out her own beat with her foot. *Almost time for my part.* Lark raised her guitar pick high in the air and lowered it on her strings, adding her own metal sound to the bright melody. She closed her eyes, swooning to the joining of two great musical styles. Crescendo. *Oh, there's that sweet spot on the guitar.*

The classical music stopped. Lark turned toward her window. Until now, she hadn't realized her large, bare office window faced Everett's large, bare office window just a few feet away. And when the lights were on, they could see each other perfectly.

Everett stood like a soldier in his suit with a no-nonsense stare. All in all, he looked pretty daunting. In fact, on the jovial scale, he was a minus fifty. But even so, he had an irresistible earnestness about him, too.

37

He held up a large piece of paper with a phone number on it. She let her guitar make a slow dying sound and placed the instrument on its stand. While still humming the melody, she pushed in all the right numbers on the phone. One ring. Two rings. *Why is he waiting?*

He finally picked up the phone. "Hi. Everett Holden. Your neighbor."

Lark had to pucker her cheeks to keep from laughing. "Yes, I can see you . . . right in front of me. Good morning."

Everett cleared his throat so loudly Lark had to pull the phone away from her ear. "Please," he began. "Please don't tell me you get up every morning at six thirty to play your electric guitar."

Okay, I won't tell you. "I guess you want me to turn down my amp. It's just that I loved your Vivaldi, and I couldn't help but join in. It's so exhilarating." She shot him her sweetest smile and waited for his face to brighten. It didn't. "But I don't think it was any louder than your music." Lark tried to stay lighthearted.

Everett moved around the room, stacking manuals on his shelves, obviously multitasking. "But your music doesn't mix with my music."

Did he actually say that? Lark wondered

what the magic words were to turn up the corners of his mouth. Maybe spreadsheets and revenues.

Then she noticed it. Tiny lacelike specs floating just outside the window. "Look. An early snow!" Still holding the telephone, Lark opened the window and stuck her head outside. Fresh, crisp air swirled around her. "Everett. Isn't this amazing? A snowfall never forecasted. Don't you just love things as unpredictable as the weather?"

Lark heard nothing from her telephone partner, so she looked back at Everett, who now wore a fixed and intent gaze. It reminded her of the glassy expression held by the stuffed, wild boar hanging in Skelly's den. She'd thought an impromptu celebration of the snow with some frothy cocoa would be fun. But Everett didn't appear to be in the mood for a festive beverage.

"Don't you like snow?" She heard his raspy breathing and wondered if smoke would puff from his nostrils at any moment. Rarely did she make anyone angry. Usually people left her presence with a hug and a kind word. The moment felt unfamiliar, yet strangely exhilarating, as if she were plummeting on a roller coaster ride.

"I like snow," Everett said. "In fact, I like

a lot of things. But right now, I'm trying to work."

"Well then, have a nice day."

"Thank you," Everett said. "The same to you."

Was that a simper? He has a chink in his rock wall, Lark thought as she let a slow grin overtake her face. But then Everett dampened her optimism by parking himself down at his desk as immoveable and cold as a slab of granite. Oh well, hope still reigned. Even granite could be carved with the right tools.

Lark gave up on Everett for the time being as the snow claimed her attention. She had to be a part of it. She headed back downstairs, slipped on some moccasins and put on a coat over her long nightshirt. Once she'd flipped on the outdoor lights, she hurried out into her backyard.

The glorious white stuff fell more heavily now, floating all around her, engulfing her in a cocoon of softness. Suddenly she realized she'd never painted a winter scene. *I should memorize this moment.*

The pristine flurries had already lighted on the pines and decorated their boughs. *And what a unique quiet.* As if the snowy splendor commanded all the rest of nature to an awed silence.

The delicate feel of the flakes on her face

reminded her of a feather tickling her cheek. Lark licked the melting snow from her lips. A gust caused the flakes to do a little tango. She raised her arms and danced with the flurries, dipping and swaying and singing. She knew God looked on, sharing her pleasure in His creation. An icy gust made her shiver, so she raced back inside, laughing the whole way up to her loft.

Everett slammed his coffee mug down so hard a three-tiered bead of brown liquid rose in the air and then plopped back in his cup. Cold, bitter brew again. He made a mental note to throw out his coffee beans and buy some caffeine pills. His concoction always tasted like crude oil anyway.

He glanced over at Lark's office window. Her light was off, so she still must be out of her office. At least she'd finally gotten the good sense to come in from the cold. He'd seen her from his window, and she'd been outside twirling with her arms stretched wide. She looked stark raving mad. *Or maybe she's simply childlike.*

It reminded him of something he and his sister, Greta, had taken pleasure in when they were growing up. Sneaking out one night to play in the first snow of the winter. The moon had come out full that night, illuminated the snow, and made it glisten like stars. They'd pelted each other with snowballs. His sister had quite a hefty pitch as he recalled. Several times they'd doubled over laughing. He hadn't thought of that moment in years. But then he remembered they'd both caught colds, and his sister had been forced to the hospital when her fever and cough spiraled into pneumonia. He knew scientifically that their sickness had not actually come from being out in the weather, but in his mind he always associated the two.

He drank a glass of water, trying to get the acid taste out of his mouth. His sister had always been fun loving, yet so irresponsible. She'd always managed to convince him to go along with her schemes. But some of her ideas for amusement were reckless. In the end, her foolish behavior had been the undoing of their family.

Everett cleared his throat and wished he could clear his thoughts as easily. Yes, there had always been a price to pay for happiness. It had become his life's lesson — joy might come, but there would be the inevitable price to pay at the end.

He stared out at the falling snow and wanted to say, "Humbug." *Maybe I need some window blinds to help with the distrac-*

tions. Mental note: Caffeine tablets. And wooden blinds. Everett willed himself not to look out his window, but even as he made his private demand, he rewarded himself with one more glimpse. Hopefully, Lark wouldn't catch him gawking.

Abruptly her office lights flickered on, and she appeared at the window, giving him a wave. She had indeed caught him staring. Heat spread across his face while she slipped on that perennial, pesky, sunny smile of hers. With her hair pulled back in a ribbon, he could see the soft angles of her lovely face. Not thinking clearly, he picked up his coffee mug and then dropped it on his bare toe. The brew sloshed all over his pant leg. *Great.* He grabbed some tissues and tried to wipe up the mess, but he did more smearing than cleaning.

Mental note: Suit pants to the dry cleaners, caffeine tablets, and very *heavy wooden blinds.* Maybe he should hire someone to run his errands for him. That way he could get even more work done. Since he'd just gotten a raise from his biggest client, he felt an unwritten pressure to give more hours and produce more work. Kind of like a treadmill that management conveniently forgot to turn off.

But the additional labor was no real

problem for him. He had almost no family left. No real friends. No obligations. Just the job. A clean and productive life.

Everett did a double click with his mouse and looked at his computer screen, which now displayed an electronic ledger. He stared at the curser. It seemed to almost mock him with its incessant winking.

He looked down at his hands. His fingers were balled into fists so tightly he could feel his heartbeat in his hands. Probably from the wrath of paying an obscene amount of money for a home which turned out to have no privacy. He glanced back at Lark's window. This time she'd disappeared again. When did she ever get any work done? And surely illustrating didn't pay much.

What was the name of one of her books? In a Giddy Pickle? Okay, so now that he thought about it, he might have seen the book back in Fayetteville. Perhaps at a bookstore and on a special display at the grocery store. Okay, maybe she *was* slightly notable. But if she were *that* big, wouldn't she be working nonstop to keep up her position and lifestyle?

Everett heard some faint squealing noises next door, so he made a casual glance over to his neighbor's window. Lark and another woman were doing that girlfriend ritual thing of jumping up and down while hugging. He shook his head and groaned.

Six

"What are you doing here? This is so great."
Lark loved the idea of sharing a snowy
morning with her best friend, Calli Dash-
wood.

"Well, you said you wanted me to surprise
you sometime," Calli said.

Lark released her from their hug. "I'm so
happy you're here. But what about the
roads? Weren't they kind of slippery?"

"I drove carefully." Calli wagged a finger.
"But did you know your door was not only
left unlocked, it wasn't quite shut?"

"Oh, dear." Lark realized it must have
been left that way all night.

"I saw your car in the drive so I knew you
were home," Calli said. "I rang the bell, but
when you didn't come, I noticed the door."

"I guess I forgot. And I can't believe I
didn't hear the bell. I'm so sorry." Lark
folded her hands together in front of her.
"Maybe I can make it up to you with

breakfast burritos and lots of homemade salsa."

"Now you're talking." Calli took off her coat and pulled out a bag of candy from her pocket. "I brought you a present. Little Chocola' Rocks from Sweet Nothings."

"Is that the candy shop you're always talking about in Hot Springs?" Lark asked.

"Yeah. And the owner, Nori, is quite the entrepreneur. The next time we go to Hot Springs I think you'd both get a kick out of meeting each other."

"I'd love to." Lark accepted the beautifully decorated bag of sweets and put it on an easy-to-reach shelf, thinking they'd be great for munching while painting or reading or just about anything. "Thanks."

Lark noticed Calli's new casual look in jeans and tennis shoes. Her friend had her hair down in dainty curls, with a few tiny braids on the sides. She had always admired Calli's tall stature, her rich, cocoa brown complexion, and almond-shaped, brown eyes. She wondered if her friend wouldn't mind posing for her someday. She'd make a great model. Lark tuned back into the conversation as Calli chatted about all the ways *not* to make snow ice cream. They clomped down the stairs together, chuckling.

After breakfast and a few hours of much needed girl talk, they settled back into the loft. Calli sat in the purple beanbag chair to peruse Lark's newest picture book, *In a Giddy Pickle.* "This is so incredible. You know, Nissa is a great writer, but your illustrations make the book. And this cover . . . so whimsical and beautiful. Kids are going to love it. Congratulations."

Lark smiled. "Thanks."

"I guess you'll have some book signings again." Calli tried to get up from the chair and fell back down. They both laughed.

Lark reached out her hand to help her friend up. "My publisher has set up quite a few over the next several months. It should be fun meeting the kids and their parents. I hope you'll come to one of them."

"I always do," Calli said. "So has this new publisher hired you for another project? They should."

"Not yet. But it's okay." Lark fiddled with one of her camel-hair brushes, making pats on her palm, pretending it was a butterfly. "I'm enjoying the break." Lark took a few mini packets of jellybeans out of her big bowl and tossed them to Calli.

"Ohh, yeah. Armed and dangerous." Calli popped a jellybean in her mouth. Then she strolled around Lark's studio and studied her paintings on the wall. "Your oils have gotten even better than the last time I was here. So much more depth and emotion. You are remarkable."

"Thank you." Lark fidgeted with her art supplies, moving her gesso and mineral spirits around from one spot to another. Watching her friend, Lark wondered why she felt so uncomfortable when people observed her artwork.

Calli milled around the other side of her studio and stopped to gaze at a still life of pears and yellow roses and then one of a Victorian village. "Now why is it you haven't shown these to anyone? There are so many terrific galleries here."

Lark shrugged. "I'm not sure."

"But that's what you told me last year. What's going on?"

"Guess I'm still not ready." Lark felt uncomfortable talking about her work beyond illustrating.

"Oh, boy. I know that's not *this* ladybug talking," Calli said, doing a little lasso gesture with her finger. "You are indomitable, girl. Why? Because God is with you, and He's given you an amazing gift here that He expects you to share. And I don't just mean your illustrations." She raised an eyebrow. "Now do I hear an Amen, sister?"

"Amen." Lark took her friend's hand and squeezed it. "Okay. I'll call one of the local galleries . . . sometime."

Calli tapped her finger on her cheek.

Lark laughed. "Okay. I will call . . . soon. I promise."

Calli took off her freshwater pearl bracelet and rolled it onto Lark's wrist.

"What are you doing? I can't accept this. It's your favorite. Isn't this the one you bought in one of the shops downtown?" Lark touched the bracelet, wondering if she should give it back. But she didn't want to hurt her friend.

"Yes, but I want you to have it," Calli said. "It looks good with your nightshirt."

They both chuckled.

"*And* I want it to be a symbol of the pledge you just made to me. A reminder. Okay?" Calli lowered her gaze as if to add an extra helping of serious.

Lark nodded. "You're the best."

"Yeah. That's what my customers keep telling me."

"You *are* the best Realtor in Springdale."

"Well, I guess I really like helping people find their dreams."

Lark held up the new bracelet on her wrist. "I can tell."

Calli glanced over at Everett's office

window. "So I guess this is the new neighbor you were talking about. What was his name again? Everest Molden?"

Lark laughed. "You're close. Everett Holden."

"Wow, look at that," Calli said. "When he has his lights on, you can see everything he's doing. I mean, your windows are so big and close, it's like you're both in a fish bowl. His profile is certainly impressive. Uh-oh. He's glancing over at us."

They both waved at Everett.

Calli whispered, "But when he smiles, it looks more like he's lifting heavy furniture."

Everett's office chair squawked in rebellion as he tilted it back. He stared at his knee. Looked like he'd picked up another tic. His foot bounced, making his leg continually jiggle. "Where did that come from?

"Maybe I'm being punished for something. And do other guys talk to themselves so much?" Of course, most men probably let off steam with their friends. But people just made life so tedious; he wondered if friendship was ever worth the bother. Everett pushed on his leg, forcing it to stop bouncing.

But on the other hand, the holidays were coming, and friends did come in handy to make things more festive. Christmas. Sure, he'd attend a client party or two and show up at a church activity, but for the last several years, the big day had been spent alone. He'd eaten foods he'd had catered and opened presents he'd given to himself. None of his life seemed dismal until now. Until he'd had a window view of the most maddening and fascinating woman he'd ever met. Larkspur. A woman who seemed to glow from the inside out. Kind of like a light bulb, only a lot brighter.

But what kind of strange air was he breathing in this neighborhood? *I don't even know the woman.* Then he remembered her holiday invitation. *Hmm. A thought: Eating over at her house would certainly save money.*

He stared back at his screen and the glaring numbers. He was always the bottom line guy. Charts and spreadsheets and graphs had always been a part of his life, but now he wondered if they had consumed him. Some people had even come to fear him at meetings because of his stern reports. Everett whispered, "I've become the bad-news guy."

He looked up and noticed his sister's music box on the shelf. He lifted the memento down and rubbed his finger along its rough, carved surface. It was one of the last belongings of hers he'd kept. He tried to rotate the little crank, knowing it wouldn't turn. Greta had broken it from twisting it over and over until she'd wound it too tightly. The box seemed to reflect her life all too well.

He then saw the licorice chewing gum Lark had given him the day he'd moved in. The packet sat on his desk, daring him to try another piece. Finally, he rolled his eyes in exasperation and opened a stick. He studied the powdery grayness of it, thinking how ungumlike it looked and then stuffed it in his mouth. He chewed for a moment. Sweet. Unique. The flavor reminded him a little of molasses. Guess you'd either really love the stuff or really hate it. No middle ground. After another chew or two, Everett tossed the rest of the packet of gum in the wicker trash bin. He missed. Who cared? Time for action.

He snatched up his keys to his brand new sedan with all the bells and whistles and headed out. Everett wasn't even sure where to go. Maybe he'd get a real cup of coffee downtown. And then later, he'd try to find the heaviest wooden blinds money could buy.

SEVEN

After a shower and a few more hours of catching-up with Calli, Lark's stomach began to growl.

"I heard that," Calli said. "Now did you mention some homemade cinnamon scones, or was I dreaming?"

Lark tugged on her friend's arm. "Come on. You weren't dreaming."

"I'm wearing elastic jeans so I can eat more than one."

They both laughed.

Just before they headed down the stairs again, Calli glanced over at a canvas sitting on an easel. "Now what is this one going to be?"

Lark paused before going downstairs. "I'm not totally sure. I've sketched in some of it. A garden with a woman sitting on a bench. But something is missing. The balance is off. It needs something . . . or someone."

Calli tapped her cheek. "Yeah. Maybe

you're right." As she gazed out the window, her eyebrows creased, making angles on her perfect oval face. "Will you just look at that?"

Lark followed Calli's gaze into her neighbor's office. *Oh my.* She flipped off her lights and watched the play-by-play as a crimson-faced Everett trudged up a stepladder to fasten some monstrous, wooden blinds to his bare office window. He struggled with the blinds as if he were wrestling with an alligator. Without warning, Everett fell off the ladder.

Calli gasped.

"Should we call an ambulance?" Lark asked.

"Wait a sec," Calli said. "Maybe he's okay."

Everett stumbled to his feet again, amazingly unhurt.

Lark and Calli sighed with relief and then sputtered some pent-up giggles.

This time Everett made it up the ladder with the blinds, a rock hammer, and some nails the size of railroad spikes.

Lark noticed he didn't look all that chipper. She shoved her long hair behind her shoulders and cocked her head. "Go ahead, girlfriend. I know you're itching to say something about my neighbor."

"Owwee," Calli said. "I love all God's creatures, but who in the world installs wooden blinds in a three-piece suit and a button-down shirt?"

"Everett *is* kind of stiff," Lark said.

Calli folded her arms. "Honey, if he were any stiffer, I think we'd have to bury him."

Lark leaned against the window frame. "But I feel sorry for him."

"Uh-oh. I can see what's coming. Sure, you've got to love them in the Lord, but repeat after me, 'Everett Holden *is* a handsome man, but he is *not* a wounded animal.' He's not that skunk you nursed back to health when you were twelve."

Lark rolled her eyes at her friend. "It wasn't a skunk. It was a squirrel."

Calli put her hand up. "I'm just messing with you. I suppose God could have planted Everett over there for a reason. Should be interesting to find out what it is."

Lark wanted to discuss the lonely plight of her hermit professor, Dr. Norton, but the time didn't seem right, so she just sent up a prayer for her new neighbor instead.

The next morning, Lark followed Calli out the back door to her car and then paused for a second to take in what was left of the breathtaking leaves. *I think the colors must get brighter every year. And they look especially pretty with a dusting of snow.* She finally pulled her gaze back to Calli. "I wish you could stay longer."

"Me, too. But I've got to show some houses to a couple this afternoon, so I'd better get going." Calli tossed her overnight bag in the backseat of her Mercedes.

"We had a really good time, didn't we?" Lark wondered if she'd ever get too old for slumber parties. She doubted it. There was nothing quite like staying up late eating a fresh batch of cookie dough while watching old black and white movies. But the best part was sharing the experience with her best friend.

"Yes, we surely did." Calli slid into her car.

Lark really liked her friend's power suit: tailor-fit, navy fabric, with a killer scarf. "Love that outfit."

"Thanks," Calli said. "Hey, come visit me. Okay? And I'll make you some homemade chicken and dumplings like my granny used to make. Best eating in Arkansas." She shut the door and started the engine.

"I know the roads are clear, but call me when you get in," Lark said. "Otherwise I'll worry about you."

Calli patted her hand on the car door.

"Ladybug, I'm not going to worry you're worrying. Cause you've never been a worrier. Besides, the sun has spun gold this morning, making the leaves into jewels. And that'll keep me awake and singing the whole way. Thank you, Jesus." Calli turned on the heat. "You're turning into an ice cube out there. I'd better say bye." She waved and pulled out of the driveway.

Lark folded her arms around her middle and bounced to keep warm.

"Now don't you go and marry that next-door neighbor of yours while I'm gone. Do you hear?" Calli hollered back to her.

Lark put her fists on her hips to try to appear annoyed with her friend but gave up when she felt a big smile spread across her face. She then waved until Calli's car was out of sight. She glanced around at the spots of leftover snow, which had become like shimmering diamonds in the sun. All was so beautiful. *Yes, Everett would miss another dazzling day laboring in his grotto.* When she turned around, she noticed a sign hanging on his front door handle. *What is that?* She shivered but just had to have one quick peek.

She took a few steps toward Everett's house and peered up on the small porch area. Now Lark could read the sign clearly.

58

DO NOT DISTURB. She couldn't believe it. Just as she tried to clamp her mouth shut from the reality of it, a van pulled up in front of his house. The name of the company was written across the van in purple and gold. GOURMET TO YOUR DOOR. COOK NO MORE. Everett was having his meals delivered? Wow. Hibernation to a new and scarier level. She wondered if he'd ever come back out for human contact. Oh well, he was a big boy. Not a squirrel. *Well, maybe a little squirrelly.*

Lark could smell wood smoke again. The scent made her think of cozy family gatherings around the fireplace, but since the cold wind was starting to seep through her sweatshirt and jeans, she scuttled back up the driveway and into the warmth of her kitchen. She immediately noticed her bowl of pomegranates on the counter. "Hmm." She grabbed a sketchbook out of her drawer.

Skelly had given her a bouquet of bougainvillea from his little hothouse, so she slid the vase of flowers behind the bowl and sat down on the kitchen stool. The petals had faded to an antique-looking peach and gave the fruit a nice backdrop. She added a tall bottle of olive oil to the scene. *Not quite right.* Less was more sometimes, but the balance looked off. A scene with an odd number of items always made a more pleasing picture though. To her, asymmetry was one of those mysteries of art. Lark glanced over at the sack of medjool dates she'd bought at the grocery store. *Okay, that might be interesting.* She added a handful to the scene. *Yes. Just right.*

Lark chewed on a date as she made some sweeping outlines of the objects with a charcoal pencil. Mmm. Medjool dates. They looked a little like roaches, but they were always so sweet and creamy.

She noticed some bad spots on a couple of the pomegranates. *Oh, well.* She'd draw them as is, blemishes and all. It reflected life, didn't it? All things lovely still missed a vital connection to glory. In fact, wasn't art of every kind reaching for something more — hoping, dreaming of knowing that Someone who was greater than oneself? Too bad some people refused to consider the grace that could reconnect them to their Creator.

Lark continued her drawing, adding shading here and there. She held it up. *Not bad.* But soon her thoughts drifted back to Everett. Maybe he was reaching for something, as well, but didn't know it. Perhaps in his case, he simply needed to be plugged back into life.

Lark fingered her earlobe, because somehow it made her think more clearly, and then out of the blue she got an idea. Just a little idea, but she thought it might have real potential. Just below her in a cabinet, she'd stored away a brand-new box of mothballs. She put away her sketchbook and reached for the box. She took some ribbon from a kitchen drawer and adorned the box with a silky bow and streamers. *Okay, pretty in an odd sort of way.*

Not bothering with a coat, Lark slipped out the front door and tiptoed over to Everett's house. No sign of the Gourmet to Your Door van, so all looked clear. She then crept up onto Everett's porch. The goofy sign still dangled from his door handle. DO NOT DISTURB. She set the box on his doorstep and rang the bell.

Perhaps the gift would come off a little startling, but she would certainly want someone to do the same for her if she'd become a workaholic recluse. Everett needed to take his life out of storage so as not to have the same tragic ending as her dear, old professor. Symbols were powerful tools, and the mothballs could be just the humorous and persuading gift to bring him to his senses. Lark hurried back to her porch, rubbed her arms to keep warm, and slid through her front door without looking

61

back. *Everett will surely thank me someday.*

She completed her task and then plopped down on her bean bag chair for the next hour to get caught up on reading her new art magazines. Just as Lark finished absorbing one of her publications, the doorbell rang. She trotted downstairs and swung the door open, hoping it wasn't Everett ready to pelt her with mothballs. But no one stood on her porch. *Weird.* Just before she shut the door, she found an out-of-the-ordinary kind of object sitting on her welcome mat. *A gavel? Why is there a gavel on my welcome mat? It's from Everett.* She turned it around in her hand. Lark smiled even though she had no clue as to what it meant.

Once back in her loft, she continued to ponder its significance. She looked out her office window and stood in amazement. The blind on Everett's window had been removed. Yes, he must have figured out the mothball gift. He'd understood its meaning, and it had changed his life. Like an epiphany. A blissful, crocodile tear rolled down Lark's cheek. Life was so good.

She believed the gavel was indeed from Everett. He had apparently decided to give her a little funny present in return. *How sweet.* But now for the riddle. What could the gavel represent? Oh, she loved a good brainteaser. *Okay. Gavels are made of wood. Gavels are used in courtrooms.* The full meaning hit her as if she'd been smacked in the mouth by a giant, slushy snowball. What are gavels used for in a court of law? *To silence those who are out of order!*

EIGHT

The computer screen glowed in front of Everett, keeping him connected to the pulse of life like an umbilical cord. The analogy felt strange and slightly worrisome to him, but some days it felt true.

Everett stared at the floor. The expensive blinds he'd purchased the day before had fallen in the weight of their own gloom and now sat in a strangled mess. He'd been glad when they'd come crashing to the floor and decided to leave them there to remind himself of what could come from decisions made in haste. He'd just have to learn to toss a wave to Lark in the morning and then focus on his work.

Everett glanced at the box of mothballs on his desk and broke out into another smile. He touched the soft ribbon tied on the box. After he'd heard the doorbell earlier, he'd brought the present inside and proceeded to waste an hour trying to figure out what the mothballs were for.

Then he got the meaning. The day of the Igor-gift episode, his jeans had been full of holes. And the mothballs were meant to be comedic in some way. Sounded ludicrous when he'd said it out loud, but he couldn't think of any other answer.

Back to the screen. Amazingly, in spite of all the interruptions from Lark, Everett had still caught up on his work. Of course, he'd worked half the night to accomplish his goals, but he'd been pleased to get a complimentary e-mail from one of his clients, praising him on a job well done.

So, in a flash of something he didn't fully comprehend, he allowed himself a moment of revelry to celebrate. He'd decided to place a gift on Lark's doorstep — an old gag gift from a party. He thought she'd appreciate the meaning. By giving her a gavel, he cleverly welcomed Lark to speak. In other words, she held the reins of speech now.

Is that the doorbell? Lark. He headed downstairs with the box of mothballs. Once at the door, he was surprised to see his principal client, Zeta, standing there on his porch. Her extra tall height loomed over his medium frame. Everett smoothed his blue tie and found his vocal cords. "Zeta? Hi.

This is a surprise. A good . . . one." He wondered if he sounded wooden or anesthetized. He'd had little sleep and no client had ever come to his home before.

"Well, so here you are. Look at this place. I wouldn't have picked this enormous dollhouse as being quite your style. But it's impressive nevertheless." The angles on her face suddenly appeared sharper, and her dark eyes took on their usual narrowing glare. "In fact, maybe we're paying you too much."

Everett tried to laugh, but it came off like a choking cough.

"Well, aren't you going to invite me in?" Zeta stuck a loose strand of black hair into her felt hat.

"Would you like to come in?" Everett knew he sounded more like Igor than a highly paid accountant.

"Maybe . . . just for a moment." Zeta stepped inside, almost pushing him out of the way, and then looked around. "Hmm. Not too bad. But why do all members of the male species feel compelled to buy brown leather?"

What could he possibly say? Everett cleared his throat.

"I brought you the file we discussed." Zeta threw her cape over her shoulder, revealing a blood-red suit. Kind of a post-Dracula look. "You were so close by, I thought I'd drop it by on my way to lunch."

Zeta pulled another frown out of her hat, but he had no idea why. He wondered if he were simply out of practice at reading human emotions since he spent so much time alone. Locked away in his office, dealing mostly with e-mail, maybe he'd lost some people skills. Or perhaps Zeta just needed some lessons in manners. He cleared his throat.

"Do you need a lozenge or something?" Zeta set the file on his entry table.

"No. I'm fine." Just as he was about to ask if she'd like to sit down, the doorbell rang again. He felt some head pain creeping in.

Zeta raised an already arched eyebrow as she stared at the box of mothballs in his hand.

Everett opened the door. Lark stood in front of him looking radiant in a light purple sweater and white jeans as she clung to a rolled up newspaper. "Hi."

Lark smiled at Zeta and then held out the paper to Everett. "I believe someone left this paper on my doorstep. It must be yours." Lark licked her lips. "Have a good day."

Everett took the paper, but wondered why Lark wasn't her bubbly self.

Zeta tapped her foot. "Are you going to introduce me to your neighbor, Everett?"

Why not? What can I possibly lose? After he'd made the formal introductions, Zeta let out a yelp.

"Are you *the* Larkspur Wendell?" Zeta clasped her hand to her throat like a star-struck teen.

Lark hid her hands behind her back and glanced down. "That's me."

Everett noticed Lark's bashfulness. *A new look for her. Kind of cute.*

"I heard you lived here in Eureka Springs." Zeta pointed her red-painted fingernail high in the air with a flourish. "Everett, why didn't you tell me you had such an illustrious neighbor?" She leaned down to Lark. "My daughter has all of Nissa's books, but just between you and me, your illustrations empower them. My daughter has drifted off many a night while looking at those fanciful pictures. Especially the *Electric Seeds* series. We have them all."

"I'm so glad." Lark backed slowly to the door. "If you'd like, I could personally sign some books for your daughter. I always keep a supply at home to give away."

Everett met Lark's gaze, but she didn't

smile at him. She stared at the box of mothballs with a forlorn kind of expression.

"Autographed books for my daughter! How wonderful!" Zeta clapped her fists together. "She'll love it. Oh, and I will, too."

"Well, I'll go and get them now. I'll be right back." Lark turned to leave and then whirled back around. "What's your daughter's name?"

"Amelia Stone. Thank you so much."

Lark hurried out the front door, while Zeta turned to Everett. "Well, aren't we full of surprises?"

Everett frowned. Even though Zeta was his most important client, he didn't like being talked to in the third person like a toddler. He set the box of mothballs on the entry table.

"So what's with the mothballs?" Zeta spoke in her usual brusque tone.

Everett swallowed his exasperation. "It's just a funny gift somebody gave me."

Zeta stood silent for a second, looked confused, and then burst into laughter. He'd never heard her laugh before. Guess he'd better count that as a blessing.

"How very clever," Zeta said. "I love it. Mothballs. Definition. A condition of being in storage. You know, you really are too much of a hermit here in your home office."

The conversation felt *way* too personal and more than annoying. Everett glanced in the entry mirror and noticed his face had reddened to a rich, tomato hue. Zeta's rudeness was more than he could stand sometimes, but he was determined to keep his cool. "Larkspur Wendell left the mothballs on my doorstep."

Zeta eyeballed him like Igor's assessing parrot gaze, and then she detonated with another round of laughter. Directed at him. Again. This brief meeting was racing downhill fast. And worst of all, he'd gotten the meaning of the mothball gift all wrong. Maybe it had been more of a putdown than a lighthearted gift between neighbors. His leg began to twitch all on its own again.

Lark tapped on his door and let herself in with a stack of books. She set them in Zeta's waiting arms. "Oh, thank you, Larkspur. May I call you Lark?"

"Yes, of course. I've personally autographed each one and added a little special note in the top one," Lark said.

Zeta's fingers clutched the pile of books as if she were afraid someone would take them from her. "You are a peach for doing this for my daughter."

Everett tuned out for a moment and then suddenly noticed the gavel in Lark's back pocket. She pulled it out and set it on the entry table with all the other assorted items.

Guess Lark didn't think the gift was witty after all. Then as she stared at him, her lovely, brown eyes softened. "Gavels are meant for silencing people. Aren't they?" Her voice sounded more hurt than angry.

Everett turned to Lark. "That's not what I —"

"Okay, I'm lost here," Zeta said. "I tell you what. You can finish this peculiarly stimulating conversation tonight. Everett, why don't you bring Lark with you to our company party? I read that Lark is single, and you have nothing important to do to-night."

"Company party?" Everett asked.

"You know," Zeta said with more than a hint of sarcasm. "Ozark Consulting?"

He'd totally forgotten. But then maybe he'd meant to forget it.

"You mean you hadn't planned on com-ing tonight at seven?" Zeta asked.

"I've been busy with the move, so I —"

Zeta touched her fingers under her chin in a dramatic gesture. "It's a stylish affair at the Majestic Hotel," she said to Lark. "I can already tell you'd love it. Then I'd get a chance to visit with you some more."

Is she arranging my dating life? He chose

71

not to lash out at Zeta, but he had to admit his job and its handsome salary were being worn down by her edges.

Lark's expression continued to soften when she glanced at him. He thought the look might be one of pity. *Please, any emotion but that one. I may look like a toad next to my boss, but I still have my pride.*

Then Lark smiled at him, a warm and effervescent one. The kind he was growing very fond of. Something thawed between them like two blocks of ice left in the afternoon sun. Everett decided to set his aggravation with Zeta aside and just ask Lark to the party. "I have to admit it's a good idea. Lark, would you accompany me to the party this evening?"

Lark hesitated and then stared at him as if trying to read his expression. "Yes. I'd love to."

Zeta stomped her foot as if she were starting up some Irish dance. "Good. It's settled. I'm off. See you lovebirds tonight."

Everett rubbed the back of his neck.

"By the way, Lark, this is supposed to be our company Christmas party. Everett suggested we schedule it in early November on a Monday evening. Saves money," Zeta said.

Everett groaned inside as he walked Zeta to the front door. With one last salute to her, he shut the door.

"I guess I'd better get going, too." Lark made a few steps toward the front door.

"I wish you'd stay for a bit." Everett wondered what was going through her mind.

Lark turned back to him and smiled. "I like your boss."

Everett could feel his head pound just thinking about Zeta. "I'd better not say anything."

Lark looked concerned. "Is Zeta really that hard to work for?"

Everett wasn't sure how much to tell her. "Let's put it this way. Before she became my boss, I had more hair."

Lark chuckled.

She actually laughed again. A bubbly kind of noise. Not frenzied, but a pleasant sound of contentment. He couldn't even remember the last time he'd made anyone laugh so much. "Would you like to sit down?"

"I don't want to keep you from your work."

"Well, I put in some long hours last night, so I'm pretty much caught up for a little while."

"Okay, then. Maybe I'll stay for just for a minute." Lark eased onto the end of his brown leather couch. She picked up a small brass abacus and studied it.

Everett sat on the opposite side of the couch. They sat in silence for a moment, until he thought of how he wanted to apologize about the gavel. "I wanted to —"

"I'm truly sorry about the mothballs." Lark rubbed her earlobe. "I thought they would be an encouragement. You know, to get out of the house once in a while for some fresh air. I was concerned about you. But it *truly* was none of my business."

"Apology accepted." Everett rested his arm on the back of the couch and then realized he'd made himself too relaxed for what he needed to say. So he leaned forward. But now he couldn't see her. *Oh brother.* He gave up and just looked at her. "The gavel represented a way to welcome you to speak. In other words, 'you hold the reins of speech now.' I wasn't thinking of the other side of the meaning. A comedy of errors here, I guess, but I do apologize."

Lark sighed. "Errors like straws upon the surface flow: He who would search for pearls must dive below."

"Dryden?" Everett asked. *Or was it Shakespeare?*

"Wow. I'm impressed," Lark said. "I thought for sure you'd say Shakespeare. College literature class I presume?"

"Yeah. Forced at gunpoint by a sweet professor lady who loved English authors. Well, I say sweet. I think she really had a broom in the back."

Lark chuckled.

Oh, how he could drink up her laugher. *Drink?* Should he have offered her something to drink? He suddenly felt as clumsy as Frankenstein trying to learn social skills.

Lark scooted to the edge of the couch and rose. "Thank you for taking the time to let us dive below the straw for pearls."

"You're welcome." Everett got up from the couch. *Guess it's too late to offer beverages.*

Lark set the brass abacus back on the end table. "I admire people who are good with numbers. You were probably born counting your toes."

Everett chuckled, and he noticed how good it felt. "I saw one of your covers when you handed the books to Zeta. It was extraordinary. Were those pictures done in oils, too?"

"No. I do all my illustrations in watercolor. My oils are something I do more for me. By the way, I like your living room," Lark said.

"Thanks." She changed the subject, and he wondered why.

"With all the stone and wood, it makes

me think of a vacation home."

"That's why I picked it." Had he been caught staring? Lark looked so beautiful today. Luminous dark hair and eyes that could wake a guy up in the morning better than any shot of espresso. Better than anything, in fact. He'd better not drift any further down that road. Dangerous territory. What had she said? Or had he been talking?

"So are you taking me to the company party to please Zeta?" Lark looked vulnerable as well as cute.

"No," Everett said. "I'm taking you to please myself." *Was that egotistical?*

"Sounds like an honest answer." Lark smiled as she walked to the door. "But I think Zeta railroaded you, so if you want to back out, here's your last chance."

"I don't want to back out," Everett said. "Relaxation tends to be at the bottom of my to-do list, but I really do want some fresh air . . . with you. Maybe you can teach me how to breathe again." Did those words actually come out of his mouth? Maybe there really was a romantic heart beating inside him.

Lark looked over at the corner of the living room where his mother's piano sat with the lid down. Then she smiled at him. "I guess I should go."

Everett opened the door for her, but he didn't want Lark to leave. He wanted to keep listening to whatever she had to say about anything. Her voice had a gentle ebb and flow to it like an ocean's tide. But duty called, especially since Zeta had brought the new files to add to his project.

"I'll pick you up at six thirty. Is that okay?" Everett asked.

"Yes." Lark stepped over the threshold, but when she turned back around, they were suddenly standing close.

"I look forward to this evening," Everett whispered.

Lark blushed when she looked at him.

The rosy color looked so good on her cheeks, he wanted to kiss the very spot he'd made warm by his words. In fact, what fragrance did she wear? Some expensive perfume, no doubt. "Okay." If he were being drugged by the scent, he knew he wouldn't put up a fight.

"Okay," Lark said.

Everett walked her home, which took all of two minutes, and then he settled into his office assimilating Zeta's file into his project like a good little accountant. Suddenly, he wondered if he could get by with a suit for the party or if he was expected to wear a tux. He couldn't even remember the last time he'd worn his tux. The goofy thing probably didn't even fit anymore. Did his sedan have enough gas? And what about flowers? Was he supposed to buy a corsage for Lark, or did that practice go out with the high school prom?

Everett looked over at Lark's office window. He couldn't see her because the sun's brightness had darkened the view inside. He tugged on the ribbon on the mothballs instead, hoping Lark was having just as much trouble concentrating as he was. *In fact, what could she be up to right this minute?*

NINE

Lark went back to her sketchbook and then switched on her French language CD. *"Bon soir!"* she repeated after the teacher. She chuckled. *Who am I kidding?* She couldn't smother the anticipation she felt about the coming evening. Work suddenly felt like going through the motions, but she still tried to concentrate on her charcoal drawing. Half an hour later on the last bit of shading, the doorbell rang.

Everett? Hope he didn't change his mind. Lark flung the door open to find Jeremy standing before her looking ruggedly attractive in his ponytail and scruffy jeans. But then he always looked that way — like he'd just gotten back from bungee jumping in the Grand Canyon. "Welcome! *Soyez le bienvenu!*"

"Thank you. Guess you're working on those French language tapes again." Jeremy rubbed his chin, which seemed to have a perpetual five o'clock shadow.

Lark leaned against the doorframe. "Would you like to come in?"

"Thanks, but I'd better get going."

But you just arrived. Lark blinked hard. "You look sort of expectant."

"Boy, I hope not." Jeremy gave her a smirk.

"I mean, did I forget something?" A sparrow flew overheard looking jittery in the cold. Lark could certainly relate.

"The teen craft fair. Remember? You're the one in charge of signing people up for the pies. Since I have my bike, we can load your Hummer."

Lark's hand flew to her mouth. "Pies? Teen craft fair. I wish I could plead amnesia."

Jeremy frowned. "You're sweet, but you're not going to be able to charm your way out of this one."

"Oh, dear. I'm in trouble, aren't I?" Lark asked. *I can't believe I forgot.*

"We've got a snag if you don't have thirty pies."

Lark smiled, wishing she could disappear. "I don't have any . . . I mean I didn't —"

"You didn't sign *anybody* up?" Jeremy's mouth popped open like he'd jumped off a cliff without the cord.

"No. But I can buy a lot of pies at the

store. I have money. How many do we need?"

Jeremy scratched his head. "Well, I have to say, one of the reasons people come is because they're looking forward to a thing called *homemade*."

"I'm so sorry. I don't think I can make thirty homemade pies by this evening."

"Not unless you're my grandmother." Jeremy wore his trademark half smile. "Okay, how about this . . . I *buy* the pies. Some good ones, and you'll owe me a dinner this week."

"You drive a hard bargain," Lark said. "Drive-through burgers, right?"

"Wrong. No junk food. I don't care where we go, but it's got to be expensive." Jeremy stuffed his hands in his pockets and cocked his head.

Lark noticed he had his usual stance when he was full of beans. "I'm being robbed here. Police!" She chuckled. "I'm truly sorry. I'm a mess about remembering things sometimes."

"Yes, you are." Jeremy shook his head. "I guess we'll need to get you some string to tie around one of your little fingers."

"Well, they'll probably want a rope for my neck when the parents find out those are fake homemade pies."

"No ropes, but there's still some tar and feathers in the church storeroom for me."

"Oh, yeah? And what did *you* do?" Lark asked.

Jeremy shrugged. "I volunteered the teens to be servers at the Valentine's banquet. Without their permission."

"Ooww. You are in so much trouble," Lark said. "And who decided to have the teen craft fair so close to the fall festival?"

"Yeah, I know. Bad move. Bet I don't do that again next year." Jeremy shifted his weight back and forth. "And so what magnificent mischief have you been up to, little lady?"

"Oh, not a lot. Just trying to coax a hermit crab out of his shell."

"And have you succeeded?"

"Maybe," Lark said.

Jeremy put a hand up. "Well, I've learned never to ask details. So I'll pick you up tomorrow night for dinner. Six. Okay?"

"On the back of your bike?" She noticed his usual scent. Eau de motor oil.

Jeremy winked. "No, we can take your Hummer. Okay?"

Lark grinned and watched as Jeremy hopped on his motorbike, revved the engine, and rumbled off with no helmet. His habit of never wearing a helmet did seem kind of reckless, but it was hard to admonish Jeremy for irresponsibility when she had just forgotten all about the teen craft fair.

Pies. Hmm. She shut the door, vaguely recalling signing up. *I wonder what happened.* She glanced at the calendar on the side of her fridge. *Yikes.* She saw the bold words in the Tuesday slot. "Pies, craft fair, don't forget," was the note she'd scrawled to herself. *Maybe I need to get my life in order.*

Lark could hear the words *How are you?* coming from the kitchen CD player and then *Comment ca va? What a good question. How am I anyway?* She felt befuddled about her apparent unreliability and even more confused about her relationship with Jeremy.

The phone rang, and Lark startled. She glanced at the Caller ID as she picked up the phone. Calli was calling from her home in Springdale.

After a few pleasantries, Lark told her all about the day's events. "But I think it all ended well. Don't you?"

"Yeah. I guess so."

"I mean he invited me to the party this evening even though I sent over those mothballs. I still can't believe I did that." Lark groaned.

"I can't either. It's a good thing he didn't

think you were crackers. What made you think of mothballs?"

"It was a spur of the moment kind of thing. You know —"

Calli made a comical huffing sound. "Before you had time to pray kind of thing?"

"Hey, are you spreading a little chastisement?" Lark sighed. "Oh well, I deserve it."

"No way, ladybug." Calli did a smacking thing with her lips. "Well, maybe a little."

Lark grinned. "Hey, what's with this ladybug stuff, anyway? Surely I'm not that flighty."

"I wondered when you'd finally ask me," Calli said. "This is a good story, so you'd better sit for this one."

Lark perched herself on a kitchen stool and waited for her friend to continue.

Calli took in a long breath. "Well, one time I was exiting off 540, and I saw this ladybug on my windshield. While I turned all my corners, it held on. No matter what happened, the sweet little thing stayed there fluttering its wings and clinging to dear life. When I got home, I held out my hand, and that ladybug climbed on my fingers and flew away as if it knew all along everything would be okay. With what you went through in your life, I guess it's kind of the way I see you."

"Thanks, Calli. It *is* a good story. Consider yourself hugged." A few tears pooled in Lark's eyes. "By the way, I sure wish you'd move to Eureka Springs."

Calli sniffled. "Find me a good man to marry there, and I guess I'd be forced to move." She blew her nose.

Lark wondered if her friend could be serious.

"Girl, now you know I'm kidding," Calli said.

"I wasn't sure." Lark stifled a laugh.

"You don't have to start setting me up with blind dates like some orthopedic queen."

Lark gasped. "I would never do that."

Calli laughed. "Well, I heard this pregnant pause, so I just thought maybe you were getting one of your little ideas."

"No, it's just indigestion from all the bean burritos we ate last night," Lark said.

After another round of laughs and some sweet good-byes, Lark busied herself by collecting acorns from the backyard. She found several dozen of the little nuts, which had been peeking their heads out of the snow. Lark gathered them up and stuffed them in the pocket of her lavender painting smock.

When she brought her treasures inside, she turned on the kettle for tea and gingerly placed her acorns in an earthenware bowl on the kitchen table. Some of the acorns were missing their little hats, but she thought those looked interesting, too, so she put them all together. After turning off the overhead light, she switched on a freestanding spotlight, which gave the acorns an oblique light of dramatic shadows. *Ahh. Perfect for sketching now.*

But her mind drifted again to the evening ahead. After all, Everett was escorting her to one of the most romantic places in town. She dropped three black currant teabags into her Victorian pot as she thought of the dress she'd wear — a floor-length emerald gown with color-coordinating evening bag and shoes. She laughed at her sudden attention to detail as if she were getting ready for her very first date.

Of course, crowds of people would be at the party. Perhaps even women who'd had a crush on Everett. *A speck of jealousy? This is so not me. Yeah, and I haven't been myself lately either. I guess attraction does that to people. Takes a perfectly sane sanguine temperament and turns her into a paranoid melancholy. Snap out of it, Lark.* She poured hot water into her little pot, letting the heat relax her face. Maybe what she really needed was a few relaxing hours at a local spa. *A seaweed mask, some eucalyptus steam, and a massage. Oh, yeah.*

The teacher on the French language tape said the next two words on her list, *roman* and *ami,* which meant romance and friend. Lark hurled an acorn at the CD player. Those two words were beginning to gnaw at her spirit whether in French or in English. They unfortunately represented the difference between Jeremy and Everett. And it broke her heart. After meeting Everett, she knew Jeremy would be just a good friend now. And no more.

Lark would always think of Jeremy as a great guy. They'd prayed together. Laughed a lot. And there'd even been a spark or two. But now she'd experienced the difference between intense fondness and what? Better not go there quite yet. Lark covered the pot with her mother's old, knitted cozy to keep in the heat. While the tea steeped, she started her sketch of the acorns.

But with Everett, the attraction and the interest were growing by the hour, and she couldn't even transpose all her feelings into plain words. If all those mysteries *could* be examined, would one even want to know? Would people truly desire to dissect such a splendid gift from God? It would be like explaining the dynamics of a rainbow.

Understanding every detail of its prismatic effects would not make a rainbow any more beautiful.

Lark poured her tea as she looked at her sketch. *Not bad so far. Perhaps better than the last one.* Maybe she could do a series of nature greeting cards using charcoal. Interesting thought. She did have a publisher some months ago who'd asked her to send some samples, but she'd never had the time.

She fiddled with the shading, smudging it, to give the picture more dimension. The steam curled up from her teacup. Black currant. Fragrant and fruity. She took a slow sip.

One renegade acorn suddenly fell away from the rest, so she placed it back with the cluster and then reflected on the day Everett had come to live on her street. She'd wondered how God would allow Everett Holden to change her life or how she would change his. It was happening, but not quite how she'd expected. She had a feeling now they'd be a bit more than friends.

Oh, phooey on the sketch. Her mind had gone to mush. She might as well shower and get ready for the evening. If she dressed early it would be as if she could make the evening come sooner. She chuckled at the silly thought.

Lark stood in her bedroom and studied her gown hanging by the closet. The breathtaking dress had a dark green, velvet bodice. Sheer silk of a paler hue flowed from the waist like a stream. She'd found the little gem on a clearance rack in Springdale, but it fit her figure as if it had been made for her. *How do you say dreamy in French?*

After Lark showered, she lifted and pinned her dark locks up in an elegant swirl. When she was in high school, her mother had taught her how to fix her hair for special dates. On those evenings, her mother brushed her long hair and hummed softly. It had felt so good and so comforting. What she wouldn't give for one of those moments to come again. *No, Lark, you're not going to let yourself cry.* She sniffled a bit. In the next breath, she hummed one of the songs her mother loved: "Go Tell It on the Mountain."

After a few more rounds of singing and lotions and primping and jewelry, she gazed into her full-length mirror at all her efforts. *Okay, not bad.* "Well, what do you think, Igor? Do I look pretty?"

"Pretty," Igor's one word was just enough.

"Thank you, Igor."

"Thank you, Igor."

Lark laughed and glanced at herself in the mirror again. Like Cinderella stepping into her coach, all was in readiness. She just hoped the evening would go better for her than it had for the fairytale heroine.

Well, now she could just sit down, twiddle her thumbs, and look over a coffee table book until Everett arrived. She eased down on the couch so as not to pull too hard on the bodice or crumple the silk. She flipped nonchalantly through a book on European castles. *Yes. Spectacular. It even comes with a moat.* Calli would certainly enjoy selling it. She'd say, "Your own unique security system." She thumped her finger on what was left of the castle's turret and then looked at the time. A little after six o'clock. *Moving right along. The castles of England. Okay.* She looked more closely at the photo of a big, brooding castle on a hill. Lark slammed the book shut. She'd never been good at killing time. It was much too valuable to waste. She just wasn't used to getting ready for a date so early or fussing over anything.

In fact, so much of her career had come so easily, she'd let herself slide into a blithe approach to life. She wondered if the ease also allowed her to slip into foolhardiness when she wasn't paying attention.

But this evening's preparations had been anything but careless. She'd taken great pains in getting ready for what she hoped would be a perfect date with Everett. Like in a fairy tale, a classic evening they would never forget.

TEN

The phone rang, making her jump. Again. *That's it. I'm going to turn down the volume on that thing.*

She decided not to rush to the phone but instead let the answering machine pick it up. But when she heard Skelly's panic-stricken voice, she jumped up from the couch and sped to the phone. In doing so, her left heel caught on the hem of her gown. She knew she could either let it rip or fall hard on her hands and face. In a split second decision, she righted herself, letting the silk rip. What an unhappy sound. Lark cringed.

By the time she'd gotten to the phone, Skelly had hung up. But she'd heard enough of the dilemma. Her beloved pet, Picasso, was out on the loose again, like a fugitive duck, nourishing Skelly's garden without his permission. Picasso was a true escape artist. She should have named him Houdini.

Okay, so what could she do now?

Better assess the damage on my dress first. Not bad. Fortunately, she had some tiny safety pins to fix it with. As she reached into the kitchen junk drawer she got an idea. Just a little idea. But it had potential. *I could just lift up my gown, go out on my driveway, and call to Picasso. I'll bet I can get him to come back in with just a gentle reprimand.*

Since she'd once shamed Picasso back into his pen with a shake of her finger and a scowl, she felt confident of her plan. She swung open the front door, and sure enough, there was Picasso happily scurrying away from Skelly as he tried to coax him in the other direction.

Okay, I can do this. Lark raised her skirts and headed outside, scuttling like a crab in her high heels. No need for a coat. She'd only be out for a minute.

Even though it was already dark outside, the streetlights illuminated the whole area. Once she'd made it to the end of her driveway, she decided to try the soft approach first. "Picassooo. Sweeety. Come on in now. You've had your fun outing."

Picasso got one glance at Lark and headed toward Timbuktu. He quacked and waddled down the street so swiftly, he'd be out of sight before long. *And just when I'm about to have the date of my life.* Oh well, it can't get any worse.

"Oh, all dressed up," Skelly hollered. "Hate to get your pretty duds all messed up. I can chase after him."

Skelly's face appeared flushed as if he'd been trying to corral Picasso for some time.

"No, please don't. You know what the doctor said about your heart."

But in spite of her cautions to him, Skelly marched down the middle of the street, his elbows swinging as he called out Picasso's name.

Then she remembered a trick she'd used with her first pet duck. Yes. She needed the convincing boom of the megaphone she'd used in her college cheerleading days. It was at least worth a try. She clattered on her heels back up to the house, found the megaphone on the bottom shelf of the entry closet, and clopped back down the driveway. Lark flipped the switch on the horn, and it squeaked to life. Suddenly like magic, she remembered the roar of the crowd from high school — the students she'd revved up to a feverish pitch. The rush of winning. She wondered if she still had it in her. She lifted the megaphone to her mouth and announced, "Okay. Picasso. This is Lark speaking. Let's bring yourself on home now.

You can do this, Picasso. Let's go. Let's go. Let's go!"

As if on some unexplainable cue, Picasso stopped in mid-waddle in the center of the street. He turned around, lowered his head, and began his descent from rapture. Skelly turned around, shrugging his shoulders at her. Then he laughed until his whole body quaked.

Hey. Kind of fun, but I hope Everett isn't watching. Probably wouldn't come off too romantic, all gussied up in velvet and rhinestones while hollering at a duck through a megaphone.

When Picasso toddled up to her, she reached down to stroke his neck. He felt as soft as her velvet. "Okay, little guy. Come on. I don't know how you got out of your cage again, but you have got to stop this. Your home is so nice and woodsy." Lark continued to murmur soft assurances as she lured him into the backyard. "It's full of your favorite treats. Isn't that right?" She reached inside the backdoor and flipped on all the backyard lights.

Picasso looked back at her with a darling expression. *Ducks are so cute.* She was such a sucker. But Picasso knew the fun ride was over. "Yes, sweetie. Time to go home." She closed the gate and secured it with extra heavy wire. There. Mission accomplished.

But somewhere in leading Picasso to the backyard, she'd forgotten to keep the flowing silk of her skirt draped over her arm. She hesitated, but knew she'd have to make an assessment. Slowly she moved her gaze downward. Some of the trim of her gown was splattered with muddy snow and white gooey duck drippings. "Picasso! You scalawag! You have ruined my first, and now probably my last, date with Everett."

As if knowing his guilt, Picasso began quacking anxiously around in his home.

"It's okay," Lark said. "Well, no, it isn't." She lowered her head, wondering how things could have gone so wrong so quickly.

The wind had picked up, and as always she had no coat on. She shivered as she trudged back toward the house. She could always put on another gown and shoes. But it wouldn't match her jewelry and eye shadow. *Get a grip, Lark. You've never cared about that sort of thing in your life. Guess I need to call Calli and have her slap me around to knock some sense into me. It's what friends are for after all.*

Okay. Focus. Another gown? *What time is it?* With lightning speed, she hurried into the kitchen and looked at the clock. Six twenty-nine. She had sixty seconds. *Oh dear.*

The doorbell rang. She popped in the powder room to look in the mirror. *Yikes.* She winced. Her hair looked like she'd been riding on the back of Jeremy's motorbike. For hours. She slogged to the door, opened it, and waited to hear how many creative excuses Everett could come up with as to why their date should be postponed . . . forever.

ELEVEN

Everett tried hard not to stare. But Lark stood there with her hair departing in several directions, none of which seemed to be the right ones. And her dress appeared soiled. A lone tear rolled down her cheek. He couldn't stand her distress a moment longer.

Within an instant, Everett came through the doorway and stood in front of her. He was close enough to feel Lark's breath on his face. *I barely know her. Would she want me to comfort her?* She didn't seem to object to his nearness, so he pulled out his handkerchief and wiped away her tears. Her skin felt so soft and her expression so appealing and feminine, he wanted to kiss her. But he didn't want to ruin the moment. "You must really love your duck," Everett said.

"You saw that?" Lark took a step back.

Everett slowly nodded.

"So what did you see, exactly?"

"Only what happened in your backyard. I heard you yell, 'Picasso! You scalawag!' And then something about him ruining your date with me."

Lark let out a tiny moan. "You could hear that?"

"Well, I was in my office, and I looked down when I heard a commotion." He smiled.

"Oh, well." Lark shrugged. "What can I say?"

"I would have come to your aid, but you already had him secured in his pen," Everett said. "Hey, you know, I thought I heard a megaphone earlier, too. Did you actually use one of those things to call him in?"

Lark nodded.

"I guess it worked." Everett noticed her blush again. He wouldn't want to take advantage of her in such a fragile moment, so he stepped back. "Would you still like to go to the party?"

Lark blew her nose into his handkerchief, sounding like a dainty foghorn. "If you don't mind me cleaning up and changing."

"Everyone's always late to these things." Everett hoped to make her feel at ease.

Lark sniffled. "I guess we could come in fashionably late then."

"Sounds good to me."

Lark started to hand him his handkerchief back and then stopped. "Guess I'd better wash this first." She hurried off into another part of the house. After a few seconds, she peeked back around the corner. "Please, make yourself at home."

Everett could feel his Palm Pilot in the pocket of his tux, even though he'd promised himself to keep it at home. *Must have picked it up without thinking.* Surely he could have disengaged himself from his world for a few hours. Guess not.

He glanced around the room at all the paintings. Lark had her signature at the bottom of many of them. Everett studied a wedding scene, which appeared to be set in the Ozark Mountains. A bride and her groom kissed in front of a quaint chapel with all the wedding party gazing on in delight. He was amazed at how much joy and laughter filled her paintings.

Then he took note of a still life of fruit. *Incredible!* It looked so visually accurate, it seemed as if he could reach in and remove one of the apples. Lark had an amazing talent. It made him think of his sister, Greta. He shook his head and moved on.

Lark had some prints of the masters on display as well as her own. He recognized the Mona Lisa. The woman certainly had an interesting expression. In fact, it reminded him just a bit of Larkspur's winsome smile.

The living room was also full of family photos. He walked over to the fireplace and picked up a framed photo off the mantle. In the picture Lark seemed to be in her late teens, and she stood between an older couple. Had to be her parents. She had her mother's eyes and her father's light, olive skin. Lark appeared cheery then, as well. Maybe even more so. Her parents held her in a close hug as if she were a treasure. Anyone could tell they loved each other very much. He wondered if Lark's parents lived in Eureka Springs and if she visited with them a lot.

Everett looked at his watch. He thought it was a shame on one of his rare evenings out he'd be forced to share his date with a crowd of people, some of whom would be strangers. The minute they'd see the dazzling Lark, they'd be slinking over for introductions. And then Zeta would want to have her chunk of Lark's time.

Funny how life changes. Only a few days ago, he would have cooked up ways to avoid Lark and, well, all of humanity in general. But something felt different inside him. Something had willingly shifted, yet he also felt the uneasy kind of mental jostling that tends to drive a numbers-junkie toward the edge. But then maybe he'd forgotten that the view outside his precise perimeters was far more interesting. Without thinking, his hand went to his heart. He just hoped Lark came with a survival guide.

Everett puttered around a bookshelf, noting the dust on the shelves and the rows of children's books. He pulled a few books out until he found one Lark had illustrated. *In a Giddy Pickle. Intriguing title.* He studied the cover and then the drawings inside. There could be no doubt; she had a God-given talent.

Lark stepped out from her bedroom and sort of swished toward him in a long dress.

Everett's hand went right back to his heart. "Oh, wow."

Once in front of him, Lark grasped the sides of her dress and swirled around in a circle.

She is a vision as they say. A beautiful apparition in blue. He wasn't even sure he could describe the radiance of the color of her dress, so he just stared for a moment as he tried to think of what to say. "Your gown. It looks like the wings of a butterfly. You know the iridescent . . . dust stuff?" *Oh brother. Maybe I should have just used an old standby.* "You look beautiful," Everett said with all the sincerity he could surrender. It must have been the right words because a lovely smile started on Lark's lips and then lit up her whole face.

"And you look very handsome in your tux," Lark said.

"Thank you. I rarely use it." He held up Lark's book in his hands. "This is brilliant."

"Thanks." She bit her lower lip and said no more.

"Do you have a coat?"

"Yes. It would be nice to wear it for a change." Lark opened the hall closet, and she handed him a black, velvet cape. Once he'd wrapped the softness around her shoulders, he wanted to hold her close, but he kept telling himself timing was everything. He stepped away to safer ground and cleared his throat again. At this rate, his throat would be sore in ten minutes.

There would be a hug and maybe a kiss or two if all went well. He hoped it would. Not just for the kiss, but because he could already feel some kind of emotional free fall coming on by just looking into those gloriously impish, brown eyes of hers. He couldn't tell for sure what he felt, but if he had any hopes of a parachute nearby with the words common sense written on it, he was hopelessly out of luck.

With his hand guiding Lark at the small of her back, he walked her out to his new sedan.

"Thanks for having your car right here and all warmed up," Lark said. "That's nice."

Hmm. She noticed. As he tucked her and her frothy gown into the passenger side of his sedan, he noticed her perfume again. *What police squad would ever need tear gas? They could just hose the criminals down with this stuff, and every last one of them would be incapacitated. Should I say that? Naw.*

Everett scooted in under the wheel and settled into the leather seat. He gazed at her and smiled. She was such a pleasure to look at it was hard to stop himself from staring.

"I was noticing your CD selection," Lark said. "I love piano jazz. Maybe it's the kind of music you should take up if you start taking piano lessons."

"Piano lessons?" He shook his head. "I don't think so. I took a few when I was a kid. But I don't play."

Lark turned toward him. "But did you like it?"

Everett couldn't remember ever thinking about it. At least not for a long time. He'd locked those experiences away with his

other family memories. "It was all right."
He recalled his teacher, Mrs. Musgrove,
bragging on how fast he'd caught on. "No,
I guess it was more than just all right. My
mind enjoyed figuring out the mystery of
it." He laughed. "That's the way I saw all
those black and white keys. Like a grand
puzzle to be mastered. And when I did,
people seemed to enjoy it."

Lark touched his arm. "So you took
pleasure in it."

Everett thought again for a moment. "I
did. But I guess my approach didn't have
much bravura." He backed out onto Whis-
pering Lane and headed toward downtown.

"Oh, but people who are good at math
can also be wonderful musicians."

"I've heard that somewhere before." *Oh,
yeah. Mrs. Musgrove.* Everett flipped on his
signal light. "So do you feel the same way
about the guitar? Like it's a brainteaser?"
He couldn't believe he was talking music.
Pretty artsy for a left-brain guy like me.

"No, not really." Lark shook her head. "I
thought it was a good way to communicate
what I felt in here." She pointed to her
heart.

Everett liked the way she expressed herself. "So do you like all kinds of music?" he
asked as he maneuvered through the wind-

ing streets, still marveling at the way the homes hugged the sides of the cliffs.

"Yes," Lark said. "But mostly I love Christian rock."

"So I noticed." Everett grinned at her.

Lark's head went down in a cute act of contrition. "I'm sorry about that."

"Well, my music was just as loud," Everett said. "By the way, you have talent. Why didn't you pursue a music career?"

"I would have loved to, but I decided long ago there were only so many hours in a life. There just wasn't enough time to do everything well. Or even two things well enough to do them professionally."

"You're right about life having a limited number of hours." Perhaps it's why he guarded his time so cautiously. Or *rabidly* as he overheard someone say at a meeting once. "Thank you for sharing some of those hours with me." Everett saw Lark do the lighting up thing again, and it energized him. With other women, he'd never said anything charming, but then again, maybe he just hadn't been motivated. Until now. He slipped a CD into the player. Piano music swirled around them like a soft breeze. "I can tell you like art," Everett said. "I guess you chose well. How did you get started?"

"Well, I got an assignment right after I graduated from the University of Arkansas, and the book became so successful, I kept getting more and more work. They were all in watercolors, which I enjoy. And then I've also supplemented my income with a trust fund as well as some of my other investments. It's worked well . . . *so* far."

"What do you mean?" Everett asked.

"I don't have as much work as I used to, so I need to make some choices."

"Career choices?" He wanted to study her expression but felt he'd better keep his eyes on the road.

"Yes. I've been painting with oils for a long time now. That's my true passion. I nearly have enough pieces for a show. But I just need more time before I let someone see them. I mean someone from a gallery, that is. Change is always a little scary." Lark smiled but without her usual enthusiasm.

"That doesn't really sound like you." Did he know her well enough to say those kinds of things? "The oil paintings I saw in your office and living room are extraordinary." *Just as you are,* he wanted to add, but thought it might sound too cheesy. "I'm not an artist, but I think you should share your gift with the world."

Lark looked at him as if he'd said something shocking. "I can't believe what you just said. It's the same thing my best friend told me." She folded her hands in her lap. "I guess I should listen. It's true, I would be free to follow my own vision rather than follow someone's text. Although illustrating has been good work." She fingered her pearl bracelet.

Everett wondered if the pearls were a gift from her biker friend.

"I'd love to know all about your mom and dad," Lark said.

Everett could tell she wasn't just making obligatory date conversation, but he would have given up his whole CD collection if Lark hadn't asked that one question. He generally didn't go out with a woman more than once or twice, so it rarely came up.

"You don't have to talk about it." Lark licked her lips. "I understand."

Everett doubted Lark could identify with his situation, but he felt it was good of her to let it go. He mulled over Lark's question again while he listened quietly to the music. He had to admit, her question had been a sincere one, and he suddenly felt compelled to give her an answer. "My parents and sister died some years ago. Car accident. Icy roads." He switched the music off.

Silence filled the car. Everett knew why

people shouldn't talk about such topics. What could be accomplished by dredging up misery? The pain needed to stay buried.

Lark reached out and touched his arm. "That's how I lost my parents, too."

"Really? What? I mean, did I hear you right?" Everett asked. *Oh brother.* He'd lost all his smooth conversation skills.

"My dad sold insurance here. He never made a fortune, but people loved him. And my mom and I were best friends. We always laughed a lot and sang songs together. Until a drunk driver snatched them away from me. The two great loves of my life gone instantly."

Everett swallowed hard. He'd had no idea. "I'm very sorry, Lark." Maybe she really did understand. At least about the loss.

"I miss them." Lark stared out the window.

Perhaps she expected his sad story in return. But if timing were everything, this wasn't it. In fact, he couldn't be certain the time would ever be right.

She smiled. "But I know where my parents are. So I try to do as they would do: grieve a little and live a lot." Lark laughed. "Believe me, that is *so* my mother." She shook her head and smiled as if she were remembering them again.

Everett tried not to grimace. How could she be so glib about it? Or had she simply made peace with the circumstances? He breathed a sigh of relief when the hotel came into view.

"I've been to The Majestic a few times over the years," Lark said. "The hotel was built in 1887, but I think it's still so lovely. Just like the whole area. Did you know we're called Little Switzerland of America, and that we're —" She chuckled. "Sorry, I get carried away."

Everett pulled under the porte cochere. "No, I just think you love living here."

"I grew up in the Ozark Valley. It's truly my home." Lark touched the window as she gazed beyond the hotel.

He wondered how it felt to have such passion for a place.

A parking attendant suddenly appeared out of nowhere and rushed over to open Lark's door. When Everett got to her side, he offered his arm, feeling good he hadn't become a total thug over the years.

Lark circled her arm through his. "Thank you."

They strolled to the entrance as two doormen opened the massive, beveled-glass doors. Elegance seemed to usher them in as they stepped into the foyer. Expensive tapestries lined the walls, and silk rugs adorned marble floors. Everett felt himself nodding his approval.

Lark gazed upward. "I love chandeliers."

Everett thought maybe she was trying to drum up some small talk.

Lark's finger tapped her cheek. "Especially ones like this chandelier." She pointed upward. "It's an original Moiré, made of a rare, hand-cut and polished quartz, reminiscent of the rock crystal chandeliers of the sixteenth century."

Okay. Guess that wasn't small talk.

"Yes, very nice." Lark winked at him.

Or is she pulling my leg? He knew he was grinning like a schoolboy, but he couldn't stop himself. After checking their coats in, he steered Lark toward the banquet room where the party was being held. Everett glanced around, casing the situation. He could smell the usual party smells — people perfumed to the hilt as well as trays of steaming food at the buffet tables. Live jazz and bursts of laughter spilled around the room.

Company parties are always such circuses, Everett thought. One minute people were being pigheaded at departmental meetings and then suddenly jovial at company get-togethers. Guess he'd become a cynic at the

111

ripe old age of thirty-five.

Okay, the big question: Who would run into them first? Oh boy, here comes Marge, the magpie. At least that was the nickname the other women at work used behind her back. But unfortunately Marge had earned it. She *never* stopped moving her mouth. Marge bounced up to them in her psychedelic dress. Somehow he felt sorry for her, but he hadn't a clue how to help her.

After the intros, Marge began her spiel. "I love your evening gown, Larkspur. Where did you buy it? Don't you just love it? It looks so perfect on you. Just like those fairy princess gowns we put on our dolls when we were little. You know, the ones with the billowy chiffon and all the little sparkles. Did you play with dolls, too, Lark?"

Everett felt a little bug-eyed, but Lark listened graciously to the voluminous questions. Eventually, his brain started absorbing the chatter as white noise. The ordeal took exactly eleven minutes.

When Marge was spent, Lark touched the woman's arm and said, "It's so nice to have someone ask me questions. Usually at parties people just talk about themselves."

Marge's chin did a shake. Was she about to rupture into tears of joy? He couldn't tell. "No one has ever said that to me before," she said with her hands gathered up to her heart. "Thank you . . . Lark."

They moved on through the crowd, leaving behind Lark's new friend for life — a woman named Marge. He just shook his head in amazement. *Oh no.* A man named Jamison Peabody moved toward them at an alarming rate. He was the guy at work who caused the fastest clearance of any break room. People ran from him like swimmers fled from jellyfish at the beach. It wasn't just the odors fermenting on Jamison's body, but the fact that he could literally corner people in thirty seconds flat. Give or take a few nanoseconds.

This is just great. Jamison lumbered over and stood right in front of them. In fact, so close, he'd burst their spatial bubble. Apparently, Jamison didn't realize his abdomen extended so far out they were close enough to do a three-way hug. Once they'd entered the point of no return, Everett made the appropriate introductions.

Jamison slimed Lark's hand with a kiss as he made a slight rap of his heels together and bow of his head.

Lark made no gestures of disgust but instead rose to the occasion and curtsied and smiled.

Jamison looked like he was going to pass

out from elation. He added a few chortles, which made him nearly explode out of his cummerbund.

"What do you do at Ozark Consulting?" Lark asked.

Jamison began the tale of his brilliant skills, how he was the mastermind behind the company, the brain of the operation and true pulse of the company. In other words, he was a computer programmer. But Everett could tell from Lark's questions, she wasn't just nodding politely at Jamison, she was actually listening.

Everett squelched a yawn but caught a point or two of the dialogue. Jamison actually had some good ideas, but his social skills were so misplaced he'd never been able to relate his ideas to anyone of importance. Maybe he could mention Jamison at a meeting or two.

Everett moaned audibly when he saw the infamous Zeta bulldoze toward them through the crowd like a snowplow.

"There you both are," Zeta said. "With Jamison?"

"Hi. Good to see you," Lark said. "You know, Jamison was just telling us of his ideas to improve bandwidth on your corporate network. You must be very proud to have such talented people working here."

Zeta made all sorts of movements with her mouth. First a look of shock, followed by a glimmer of revulsion. After a brief sputter of confusion, she settled on what all big shots liked to land on. Awareness. "Of course, Jamison is very good. I always keep alert of new talent." Jamison then shook hands with Zeta, said something miraculously quick-witted, and walked away a new man.

Life was full of surprises. At least it was while standing near Lark. Maybe Everett really needed to just buy a ticket and watch from the stands. But for now, his mouth felt like paper. The rough parchment kind. "Would you like something to drink?"

"Root beer, please." Lark smiled. "Lots of ice."

"Oh, icy root beer sounds *so* yummy," Zeta said. "But I'm afraid I'm dieting. Definition: eating flavored air."

Zeta released one of her laughs, and Everett willed himself not to cringe. In fact, he decided to take the high road and smile at her.

"Nothing for me." Zeta shot Everett a cagey look.

"Okay." He noticed when Zeta opened her mouth, her bright red lipstick stuck to her canine teeth. He decided not to take that one any further in his mind.

Everett tromped away, deliberately straightening his shoulders. *Great. I get the evil eye for the kind act of offering a cool beverage.* That's Zeta. The woman who had made his professional life *miserable*. Definition: to be made exceedingly uncomfortable. Kind of like trying to hug a porcupine.

Somebody he knew said, "Hey. How's it going?" Everett was about to tell him, but the guy just kept on trucking toward the food tables. Oh, well. What did he expect when he hadn't spent any real time chewing the fat with these people before?

When Everett had finally made it through the drink line, he stood there for a moment observing Lark from a distance. A few days before he wouldn't have thought to leave a fellow human being alone with Zeta, but somehow he knew all would be well. Lark could handle herself better than he could. She seemed like some elfin creature from those animated movies he watched as a kid. Lovely. Mischievous. Magical. Maybe he was good at romantic feelings when he had something to work with.

Uh-oh. Why did Zeta look so ecstatic, and why was Lark hugging her again? Zeta appeared to be crying. What in the world was happening over there? Should he barge in, or let the scene play itself out?

Everett took a sip of his cold sparkling water. He wished he could pour it over his head instead. He hadn't realized until now how exhausted he felt from worrying about losing his biggest client as well as his big salary. "The more one gains, the more one has to lose," his father used to say. And he certainly had a lot to lose.

But no matter the status of his coffers, he'd had about enough of Zeta. Surely he could express his views without getting fired. Some way to keep her from reducing him to a sniveling fool. He strode toward them as his hot hands gripped the cold glasses. Warning bells went off in his head. The pile of bills at home needing to be paid came into his mind's eye. *You're a Christian. Don't say anything rash. Nothing you'll regret.*

The second Everett arrived in their midst, Zeta threw her arms around him. His arms rose in the air to keep the drinks from spilling. The expression on his face must have looked peculiar. He would give a sizable chunk of his income to know exactly what Lark had done.

"I guess I'd better explain," Zeta said as she disengaged. "I've wanted to quit my job for ages. I already had my resignation written, but I just wasn't quite ready to mail it.

All month I've had confirmation after confirmation. And now Lark has just given me yet another one. It's finally time to leave this miserable job and live my dream. So I quit." Zeta revved up her machine-gunfire laugh again, and Everett thought it was the most inspiring and lyrical sound he'd ever heard.

TWELVE

Amidst the shock of it all, Everett lost the motor control in his fingers. The drinks fell out of his hands and crashed to the floor, sending wetness and shards of glass across the carpet.

Suddenly, men in crisp, white outfits came to his aid. They seemed to emerge right out of the mirrored walls and within seconds had whisked away all debris with a broom, dustpan, and mop.

Zeta took in a deep breath. "Well, I guess my announcement comes as a bit of a surprise to *some* people." She laughed, only this time she sounded more ladylike. "My vision has always been to open a day spa, but I always got sidetracked with making money instead of doing what I was born to do. I've saved a fortune, and now it's time to take a chance. To live!" Her voice had escalated to the point of drawing a small crowd.

Everett shook Zeta's hand and wished her the best. He'd no idea she hated her job, but it must have explained her unpleasant attitude.

"And so now I must take my leave." Zeta's hands went up in a flourish as she made a theatrical exit out the doors like an aging actress on her last curtain call.

Everett felt grateful he had nothing else in his hands to drop. He stood in stunned silence along with Lark and a few of his coworkers. They mumbled words of surprise and relief. He tapped his face.

Lark took told of Everett's hands. "Are you okay? You look a little pale."

He looked at Lark but wondered if he was really focusing. Who was this woman? The night suddenly had a *Twilight Zone* kind of feel to it. Really good, but really weird. What a strange marvel had appeared in his life.

"I had no idea Zeta would do what she did," Lark said. "One minute I was telling her what a good time I had at one of our spas, and the next moment, she was crying. I hope you're not upset with me."

Everett opened his mouth to talk, but nothing came out. He felt overcome with gratitude. He hadn't lost his biggest client, only Zeta.

"Maybe we need some fresh air," Lark said.

Sounded good. Everett hurried back for their coats and then escorted her right through the French doors and out into the garden. It was time to give Lark a big kiss or a large amount of cash. Whichever she'd prefer. He kept them walking until they were alone. The full moon dazzled the night sky, the fountain burbled and splashed, and he couldn't remember the last time he'd felt so good. "Who *are* you?" Everett laughed.

"I am Larkspur Camellia Wendell." She seemed to enjoy his odd question. "My mother loved flowers."

"I guess so." He stepped closer to her. "It's a *beautiful* name." He needed to come up with a new word besides *beautiful. Mental note: Buy thesaurus.*

"Thank you. I like your name, too. And your parents and grandparents must have liked it, too, since you are the third. Did everyone end up calling you Junior?"

"No. They tried. But I put a stop to it. Too infantile."

"I agree," Lark said. "So are you wanting to name your son Everett Holden IV?"

"No. It wouldn't even be a good name for a dog, let alone a kid." He'd never understood the need for male family members to have the same name. It reminded him of dogs marking their territory. It was a ludicrous custom.

"So . . . do you like . . . kids?" Lark fingered her earring.

Everett thought for a moment. A long moment. Slowly, he nodded. "Yeah. I like kids. Always thought maybe I'd want a couple someday."

"Yeah. Me, too," Lark said. "I'm curious about something else. Did you have a dog growing up?"

"Boy, and I thought *I* had all the questions." Everett smiled. "Yeah. I had a dog when I was a kid. But I've never had one as an adult." He put his hands in his coat pockets. "They require a lot of attention."

"And that's why Igor is living with me instead of you?"

Everett nodded. "I'm sorry. I don't have a lot of time for a pet."

"Well then, what makes you think you'd have time for a child?" Lark teased.

Oh, didn't she have all the piercing questions? Everett took in a breath of air. "It's a matter of priorities, I guess. Pets aren't a priority for me. Children would be." He suddenly wondered how committed he was to those words. She seemed bent on having him think through his whole life-agenda in one evening.

Lark gave him a smile. "Since you're busy, I'm so glad you had time to talk to me."

"Well, I guess I hoped there'd be a bit more than just talk." *Did those words actually come out of my mouth?*

Lark's mouth came open in surprise. "Are you flirting with me, Mr. Holden?"

Everett wondered if his timing was off. "Maybe a little."

"Maybe you'd better tell me about your objectives so I can decide if I approve." Lark pretended to straighten his bowtie.

He decided to throw caution to the wind and just say it out loud. "Well, I'd like to kiss the palm of your hand." *Did that come off nerdy or appealing?*

"That's honest." Lark fluttered her eyelashes. "Permission granted."

Everett reached for her hands and held them for a moment. Warm and soft. The way he imagined them. He brought one of her hands to his lips, slowly turned it over, and did just as he'd promised. When he looked back at Lark's face, she had a contented expression. "I guess I didn't answer your question from before. I'm not upset with you about Zeta. I won't lose Ozark Consulting as a client just because she's leaving."

"I guess you don't seem too upset." Lark grinned.

Everett stared at her lips. "In fact, you seemed to fix my life tonight. As well as Zeta's. How do you do that?"

Lark stepped back as if trying to regain her composure. "I'm just being me. It's what my mother always said. 'Just be yourself, Lark. Love people, and most of the time, they will love you back.' "

"And has it been true?" Everett asked.

"Not always. But enough."

Everett watched Lark as she moved her cape aside to touch the petals of a rather delicate-looking flower that had survived the freeze. Some of the fabric on her dress billowed outside her velvet cape. The gauzy material stirred around her in a breeze, making her look more like a fantasy than anything real. He thought she must have lived a pretty sheltered life. But he didn't want to spoil a really good moment, so he let it go.

"What will happen now?" Lark asked. "Do you know who your new contact at Ozark Consulting will be?"

"Well, I guess Bard Langley would be up next for Zeta's job. And that would be a good thing because we've always gotten along well."

"I'm glad for you."

Yes. I'm very glad for myself, too. He had this sudden urge to buy something for Lark. A boat or a house . . . or a diamond ring. *Come on, old boy. Not ready for that one yet.* But he *was* ready for a kiss. And this time not the palm of her hand. Without wasting another minute, Everett traced a finger down her cheek. He then leaned over and brushed his lips across her face.

Lark's eyes drifted shut as he moved his mouth over hers. His heart rate sped up as if he were sprinting. *That's never happened before.* In spite of the cooling air, Everett broke out into a sweat. *Am I having a heart attack? Mental note: Better make an appointment for a stressed EKG.* But whatever was happening, he didn't want to let go of Lark. He held her close as she lifted her arms around his neck. Her breathing changed tempo, and he wondered if she were experiencing the same sort of alarm bells.

Then a floating sensation washed over him as if he'd been set adrift in a small boat. Well, floating felt better than a heart attack. From somewhere in his head an old mantra came back to taunt him. *Passive resistance and neutrality. I can't believe those were my words concerning this dazzling woman in my arms.* Whatever resistance he had left was asked to leave.

When the kiss ended, Lark looked dazed, almost breathless. "That was the most wonderful kiss I've ever had," she said.

Everett felt pleasantly startled. He wondered if people on first dates were supposed to reveal their private thoughts. "Really?" he asked, without thinking.

"Electrifying." Lark looked down as if she were suddenly a little embarrassed.

"You mean like touching a light socket?" He grinned.

Lark laughed. "No."

"Yeah, well I had this fast heartbeat thing going," Everett said. "And it certainly doesn't seem cold out here anymore."

"Well, I wouldn't kill you if we kissed again, would I?"

"I guess there's one way to find out." He leaned in for a bit more of the sweet stuff.

When Everett released her, Lark looked at him as if she were trying to read his thoughts. Without either of them saying a word, they both sat down on a nearby bench. She looked up at the moon.

Everett followed her gaze.

"It's so lovely. What do *you* see, Mr. Holden?"

"Well, I suppose there are seas, craters . . .

scars." Everett wondered what she meant. "You know, moon parts."

"Close your eyes," Lark said.

Everett hesitated and then complied with her request. The sounds around him changed. He could hear her breathing. Soft. Steady. Then he felt the tiniest kiss on each eyelid. *As delicate as a breeze. That felt pretty good.* He opened his eyes again as she sat back down.

"What else do you see, Mr. Holden?"

Everett looked up at the moon and then followed its radiance to her face. "You glow from the reflection. You look like a guardian angel."

"You do, too." Lark kissed his cheek and smiled.

A gust of cold air whistled through the pines. "Let's go back inside." After another brief kiss, they headed toward the party.

Once inside, Everett noticed people were staring at them. *Has something else happened? Or could it be because Lark looks so — new word — spectacular in that blue dress?*

"Are you hungry?"

"Very," Lark said.

"All right. Let's go for it."

"While you're waiting in line, do you mind if I check my lipstick? I think it's been mussed a little." She grinned.

"It looks perfect, but I'll be right here in line." The moment Lark left his presence, Sylvester Markus, the owner of Ozark Consulting, barreled over to him. Sylvester leaned in to talk quietly. "Well, I guess you heard about Zeta. A day spa." There was an awkward moment, and then a blubbering bout of laughter. "You've been a first-rate contractor, my boy, and so I wanted to talk to you about becoming an employee here. You could take over Zeta's position, and it would mean a hefty raise. So I'd like to see you in my office tomorrow morning," he said. "What do you say?"

"All right." Everett tried not to overreact, but he gave the man plenty of affirmative answers even though he had to dodge his spit as they continued to talk.

After Sylvester walked away, Everett's mind reeled with the news. Hadn't he secretly hoped to have a more permanent position there? He glanced around, eager to spot Lark, to tell her about the offer. Suddenly, Everett heard a slapping noise. One of those loud, cracking ones like in the movies when a woman slaps a man. *Surely not.* But rumors were that Sylvester's hands could be a bit nomadic with the female personnel.

A few people gasped. The small crowd parted. Everett stared at the sight. Lark appeared flushed as a mortified Sylvester put his fingers up to the red handprint on his face.

Lark strode over to Everett, looking upset. He placed a reassuring arm around her as he frowned his disapproval at the very man who appeared to control a big part of his professional life. Sylvester. What a terrible turn of events.

He wanted to raise his voice at Sylvester, but unfortunately, people were waiting for that very reaction. The party atmosphere and music died out. He could hear their murmurings, and they wanted blood. Or at least a scene of some kind. But there wasn't going to be an ugly spectacle. Just a promise.

Everett raised his head. "I will not be coming to your office tomorrow to talk about a job or a raise," he said to Sylvester. "In fact, if this is the kind of sordid behavior promoted at Ozark Consulting, consider our contract terminated."

THIRTEEN

Lark gasped. "No," she whispered.

Everett offered her his arm. She hesitated and then finally circled her arm through his. *Why would Everett do this?* Granted, the man who pinched her was obviously a womanizer and deserved to be punished, but not like this. And did Everett say something about declining a job and a raise? How could this be happening?

Lark could barely contain herself. She wanted to put everything back the way it was. Right now.

She walked arm in arm with Everett through the crowd and watched it part like the Red Sea. Their stride toward the main doors didn't let up, but she could hear voices in the crowd. "Way to go," some guy hollered. And then a woman's quiet voice not far from them said, "Thank you, Everett." The only negative comment along the gauntlet was an almost whisper, "You'll be sorry tomorrow." Or maybe it was the voice screaming in her head. Her heart sank. She'd dreamed the evening would always be remembered. How brutally true that wish would turn out to be.

Once outside in the foyer, Lark pulled away from Everett. "I've kept quiet because I didn't want to embarrass you, but you can't do this. I won't let you."

Everett led her to a secluded alcove that was surrounded by tall palms. "It's already done. There's no turning back." He folded his arms. "And I don't regret it. Granted, I didn't really plan on losing my biggest client tonight, but Sylvester has been harassing women for a while now. Someone had to speak up."

"But you said something about a job there and a raise. Did Sylvester offer you Zeta's job?"

"It doesn't matter now. It's the right thing to do."

Lark noticed a flicker of something in his eyes. Could it be doubt? Regret? Who knew? She couldn't fully discern his heart. But she did know it was the most heroic thing any man had ever done for her. "I shouldn't have slapped him. Maybe I could have just growled at him or said something fierce."

Everett laughed. "I don't think you have a

fierce bone in your body."

"Well, I guess I have a fierce slap," Lark said. "It's just my mother always taught me to defend myself if a man ever tried to take advantage of me."

"Remind me to be careful," Everett said lightly.

"You've lost so much. Would you please be serious?" *Those are some pretty curious words coming out of my mouth.* People had been lecturing her on that same subject for years.

"Lark." Everett sat down in one of the overstuffed couches and looked up at her. "I don't want you to —"

"I am so sorry." Lark felt a panic surge through her — an emotion she wasn't used to.

"No." He shook his head. "I should be apologizing to you for bringing you to a party where —"

"Honestly, I had no idea that man owned the whole company." Lark glanced around to see if they could be heard. A group of people stopped near them and then walked on by.

Everett took hold of Lark's hand. "You're not hearing me. It doesn't matter who Sylvester is in the company. He has no right to manhandle my lady friend or any woman.

Am I right?"

Lark sat down next to him. "What will you do now?"

"Well." Everett released her hand and locked his fingers together. "Look for some more clients through my network." He looked back at her. "And . . . pray. It's time I took my faith seriously again." Everett let out a long breath of air. "Come on. Let's get out of here. I'm still hungry. Are you?"

Lark nodded, but what she really wanted was to help Everett. To hear him work out his frustration from the evening — to talk about his future plans if he chose to share them with her. And she needed to make sure all was well between them. It mattered to her. Now for some reason, it mattered more than ever.

FOURTEEN

Lark woke up the next morning with a pounding headache, a pain she rarely suffered. She rolled over in bed like a sack of potatoes. The sun streamed in through the shutters in bright sprays, but her disposition felt far from sunny. The big clock read nine. She'd never slept so late in her life. But today felt different. If the day had a taste, it would be soured milk.

Her foul mood certainly couldn't be blamed on Everett, but on herself alone. The rest of the evening had gone very well. He'd taken her to a fine restaurant and treated her like a princess. They'd stayed out until midnight talking and laughing. She discovered him to be a Christian man of excellent character. And in her mind, a hero, too. The fear of him becoming a permanent recluse seemed almost absurd now. But a dark shadow still circled over them like a vulture waiting for disaster. Waiting for

Everett to notice his date had ruined his life. And why? Because she sometimes tended to act impetuously and foolishly and . . . surely something else. Oh, yeah. Irresponsibly.

Lark turned over and groaned. What must she look like wallowing in childish self-pity? Her mother would say, "Have a cup of Earl Grey and then reach out to somebody who needs your help."

Suddenly her last thought triggered another memory — a nugget of wisdom from her mother on the subject of love. When Lark was young and confused about beaus, her mother would say, "You know, honey, you'll know when you're falling in love. You'll feel so many new emotions all at once, it'll feel like love is putting you together and tearing you apart all at once. You'll know. I promise."

Oh, no. It couldn't be. Could it? And she hadn't even known Everett for a full week. How could it happen so fast? What should she do now? "Mother."

Igor hopped in his cage and squawked, "Moth-er."

"Ohhh." She rolled over and groaned again. What had Everett called her? His lady friend. It sounded so old-fashioned, she wasn't sure what it meant. So was she his friend or his lady? Big distinction.

She opened one eye since the other one was plastered on the pillow. Even her ultra-soft, Egyptian cotton sheets couldn't smooth out her mood. And then it hit her. She could paint, play her guitar, eat ice cream, talk to God, and call Calli — a few things that could get her out of her slump. But maybe God wouldn't appreciate the order she'd put them in. *Maybe I'll try the last three first.*

Lark crawled out of bed as she sent up her usual praise, confession, and requisition to heaven. Then she wrapped herself up in her chenille robe and dragged herself into the kitchen for some serious comfort food — mocha ice cream with dark chocolate chunks and caramel swirls. It had been suitably named, Mocha Madness, and it would always be her favorite. She grabbed the portable phone, pressed Calli's number in, and slumped down on the floor with a ladle and a fresh pint of Mocha Madness.

"Calli Jefferson speaking."

"Hi, Calli. Do you have a minute? It's me." *It's so nice to be able to just say, "It's me." Now that's a comfortable friendship.*

"What's up? You sound kind of . . . I don't know . . . different. How did it go with your neighbor, the mothballs, and the party?"

"Long story. Got a few weeks?"

"Well, my commode just overflowed, my housekeeper just quit, and I've got two closings in half an hour, so can you lay it on me in five minutes?"

"I'll take it." Lark proceeded to quickly unload all her story to Calli. The party. The kiss. The now infamous slap. Everett's heroism. The whole enchilada. When she finished her tale of woe she stuffed a shovel of ice cream into her mouth while Calli absorbed the shock.

"Oh my," Calli finally said. "Oh my, my, my, my."

"Got any other advice?" Lark asked, talking with her mouth full and tapping the ladle against the carton.

"I don't know," Calli said. "I'll have to pray about this one."

"What if Everett had to move away?" Lark suddenly realized how telling those words were.

"I think something else is going on here." Silence.

"So *that's* it," Calli said. "You're falling in love with him. Well, all I can say is you must have really loosened up this guy or he's got you under some sort of spell."

"I think a little of both." Lark took another bite. Buttery caramel and mocha flavors sort of caressed her mouth. *Oh yeah.* Lark belched and then hiccupped.

"What in the world? Larkspur Wendell, are you under the influence of Mocha Madness?" Calli said. "Put that ladle down. You know if you eat ice cream all day, the dairy is going to make your neck glands swell up like a chipmunk. I won't let you do this to yourself."

"Okay. I won't eat another bite." Lark set the carton down on the end table.

Calli sighed. "You know, Jeremy might take this pretty hard. I know you guys have just been going out as friends, but I think he might feel more than that."

Yikes. Jeremy. I owe him supper. "Oh, Calli. I have a date with Jeremy tonight. Sort of. Another long story. What am I going to do?"

"Lord," Calli prayed, "I lift up my sister, Lark. Bathe her in wisdom and let peace and victory be hers in the name of Jesus. Amen."

"Amen, sister." Lark smiled.

"Call me later," Calli said. "I love you, sister-gal."

"Love you, too. And thanks."

The moment Lark hung up, she heard a rapping on her front door like a woodpecker. She tightened her heavy robe and then took a look at herself in the entry mirror. *Wow.*

Major damage. She gazed through the peephole. Her neighbor, Skelly, stood on her porch looking upset. *Picasso? It's impossible. He couldn't have gotten out again.*

Lark opened the door. "Skelly? Is everything okay?"

"I don't think so." He was dressed in an old, wrinkled shirt, and he wasn't wearing a coat or a smile.

"What is it?" Lark reached out to touch his sleeve.

"Well, today is my wedding anniversary. First one since Rose died. And I don't know whether to grieve or celebrate. Do you have any Earl Grey?" Mist filled his eyes.

Lark hugged Skelly. "Come on in. I have a huge supply of Earl Grey. And my kitchen is always open."

Skelly walked in, looking a little older than he had the week before. He didn't stand as straight, and he appeared thinner. He looked like he needed a little more than tea. He needed some real food, but she knew he wouldn't accept anything unless she ate, too. So while Skelly settled in with her newspaper at the kitchen counter, she snuck out her frying pan from below the stove and a carton of eggs from the fridge. "I haven't eaten yet, so will you have some eggs with me?"

An anxious frown crossed Skelly's face. "Well, as long as you're having some." Lark decided to whip up some of her best scrambled eggs. Once they were almost folded to perfection, she lowered the bread in the toaster.

Skelly insisted on helping, so she let him make the tea. He and Rose must have drunk a lot of the beverage because he seemed to know what he was doing. Lark set out some muffins from the local bakery and some pear slices, hoping Skelly would eat. When they'd sat down, Lark prayed out loud over their food and thanked God for the many good years of marriage Skelly had known with Rose. And she prayed the Lord would hold him close as he mourned his great loss. "Amen." *What a baby prayer,* Lark thought. Why couldn't she pray those steeple-raising prayers like Calli did? When her dear friend sent up words to heaven they seemed to move mountains and truly encourage the saints.

"Thank you," Skelly said. "That was a mighty good prayer."

"You're welcome." *Well, maybe God can use baby prayers, too.*

"This looks good." Skelly took a sip of his tea. "Rose was a fine cook, too, and I liked helping her. In fact, we took some cooking classes together. But preparing food for myself just isn't any fun. In fact, not much of anything is fun without Rose."

Skelly paused with a wistful expression and then took a bite of the scrambled eggs. "I know your secret, Missy. You folded real whipping cream into the eggs. Rich and creamy. They're good." He ate some more of his eggs and toast. But when he reached for a pear his arms dropped to his side. "I can't pretend anymore."

Lark touched Skelly's arm but said nothing. He felt so thin she wondered if he'd been eating at all.

"Things really aren't going well," he went on to say. "I've been having panic attacks in the night when I wake up without Rose by my side. I've never had anything like that in my whole life. I didn't even know what had happened to me until the doctor told me what it was. People tell me it's okay to grieve. But I don't want to. I just want my Rose back." Then Skelly was overwhelmed with heaving sobs. His hands covered his face as if he were embarrassed. One of his tears fell on her hand.

Lark knelt down beside Skelly. She really didn't know what to do, so she begged God to help her say the right words. Just as she'd finished her silent prayer, her mind went blank. Tears came instead as she just wept with Skelly. He patted her head, and they cried until the eggs had gone cold.

After they'd both cleaned up their faces, Lark prayed silently for a way to help Skelly. Then gradually she got an idea. Just a little idea, but she felt it was an inspired thought this time.

Lark picked up her acoustic guitar from a stand she kept in the laundry room and said, "You know, I've been working on a love song for about five years. It never had a title, but now I know why. The song should be called Rose."

Skelly put his fingers to his lips as if to stop a fresh flood of tears. "Will you play it for me?"

Without another word, Lark set the guitar on her leg. She felt the cool smoothness of the wood against her hand and then reached up to gently pick out her song of love. She'd never known where the tune had come from or why the lyrics had meant so much to her, but now it seemed as if all of the words and all of the notes had come together all these five years for this one moment in time. It was for Skelly. To celebrate his love. And to heal his heart. She finished her gentle picking as she sang the chorus one last time:

Sing now our love song,
   That's echoed through the years,
Words so sweet and clear.
   I loved you, Rose,
And I love you still.

The name Rose fit so perfectly tucked inside the chorus, Lark smiled. God's mercies had a way of making little miracles like that happen. Just when life's mosaic appeared to be no more than misfit pieces, then the Almighty offered a hint of heaven. A glimpse of the magnum opus. A foretaste of knowledge that all worked together for good and each life had a reason for being.

This moment matters to God. She must have said the words out loud, because Skelly nodded. It *all* mattered. Skelly's tears. Everett's courage and loss. Her own uncertainties about the future. Something warm returned to her heart, bringing back the glow. Her mother's words had rung true. "A little Earl Grey and somebody else's needs." Lark set her guitar back on its stand and prayed she, too, could know a lifetime of love like Skelly and Rose. Instantly Everett's face came to mind. She patted Skelly's hand. "Are you all right?"

"No . . . but I feel *better.*" Skelly said. "Thank you for the song. It was perfect for this day. If Rose heard it, I know she thought the same. Are you really going to name it after her?"

"Yes." And then Lark got another idea, but she wasn't sure if it felt inspired or was budding up from enthusiasm.

"I have a question for you. It's big one." Lark sat back down. "And you can say no if you want to."

Skelly nodded. "Fair enough. What is it?"

"Could I pay you to be my chef tonight? I have promised Jeremy a nice meal. I owe it to him because . . . well it's kind of a long story. In fact, my life seems to be full of long stories lately. But I wondered if you would enjoy doing that? You can fix anything you like."

Skelly clapped his hands together. "I'll even *serve* it to you both. It'll be fun, and it'll get me out of the house for a change."

"But since this is a special day for you, maybe we should be serving you," Lark said.

"But I enjoy the cooking more than the eating. And I don't want you to pay me, just the money to buy the food. Is it a deal?"

"Okay, it's a deal."

Skelly started to say something then shushed himself.

"What were you going to say?" Lark asked.

"Oh, nothing. None of my beeswax."

Skelly shuffled his feet. "Well, you know, I like Jeremy. He's a good youth minister, but he's not your type."

"And so who exactly is my type?" Lark tapped her finger on her arm in pretend irritation.

Skelly grinned. "Well, our new neighbor might be your type if he's a nice Christian boy. Which I think he is."

"And why do you say he's my type?" She couldn't imagine Skelly paying so much attention to her romantic interests.

"Everett is kind of a simple guy. Intelligent, but simple. He's like the beginnings of a compost heap. You know, leaves and dirt. And you're like all the other goodies that get thrown in it to make it good."

"You mean like egg shells and animal dung?" Lark asked, trying not to chuckle at his off-beat example.

"Okay, so the analogy breaks down a little." Skelly's face brightened. "You are so funny. And see? That's part of the goody getting thrown in. Don't you see it?"

"I get what you're saying. But what is Jeremy then? Is he the dung or the dirt?" Lark asked, laughing.

Skelly chuckled so hard it made his body jiggle.

Lark felt for the handkerchief in the

pocket of her robe. The one Everett had given her to dry her eyes when she'd ruined her gown. She pulled it out just enough to see the initials, E. M. H. She suddenly wondered what the *M.* stood for. *Milhouse. No way. Milroy. Is that a name? Milton. Too old. Millard. Sounded like a duck. Montague. Too Shakespearean. Montgomery. Maybe.* Lark came to herself and realized Skelly must have caught her drifting by the smile on his face. Thankfully he was too polite to mention her lapse or the handkerchief she clutched tenderly but possessively. "So you're sure I won't marry Jeremy?" Lark asked to get the conversation going again.

"You won't, my dear friend, because that is all Jeremy will ever be. A dear friend. Like me. But he will discover friendship is a good thing, too." Then he put his hand in the air. "Well, I am so outta here as you young people like to say." He headed to the front door. "Seriously, I'll be here with groceries at four thirty. Sharp. Oh, and I kind of busted up my pots and pans, so do you mind if I borrow yours?"

"I don't mind at all." Lark handed Skelly two fifty-dollar bills. He waved them in the air and headed down her front walkway. He still looked tired, but at least he had a little more spring in his step.

As soon as Lark shut the door, she wondered what Everett was up to. Would he be busy making phone calls? She hated to bother him because it'd been her fault he needed to spend the next few weeks pounding the streets for clients. Knowing she'd had a hand in truly messing up his professional life made her nearly ill, but every time the reality tried to bring her down, she gave it back to the Lord to deal with.

Once she'd showered and dressed in her favorite pink velvet overalls, she settled back in her office. Lark sat down and pretended to work at her art table. She hated to just stand up and gawk and pound on the glass, so she turned her swivel chair ever so slowly as she glanced into Everett's office window.

What? Lark rose so hastily, the chair zoomed out from under her, making her tumble to the floor. After scrambling to her feet, she blinked her eyelids to make the scene in Everett's office disappear. But it refused to go away.

FIFTEEN

A woman. An attractive blond stood next to Everett in his office. In fact, the woman had positioned herself so closely to him, even the thinnest résumé wouldn't fit between them. Guess it wasn't a job interview.

Should she open the window and toss something to get their attention? Like a sofa? But did she have the right to stop Everett? Her last thought gave her pause. She and Everett weren't engaged. They hadn't made any verbal commitments. Yet there seemed to be such an amazing bond between them. Such a hope for greater things to come. Soon.

Lark stared at them again. She couldn't see perfectly, but since his lights were on and the day was cloudy, she could see well enough. Everett seemed to take the woman by the shoulders and gently move her away. He glanced out his window and looked in her direction. Lark stepped away from her window. Since her lights were off, perhaps he hadn't seen her glaring at them.

Suddenly Everett's lights flickered off, and both of them disappeared into another part of the house. Lark felt like a sleazy private eye, and the emotion did not suit her. She also felt a bit hoodwinked. Who was this woman?

Lark had never been one to carry on over a man. But Everett had changed her heart. He had changed everything. And apparently her heart had soared before she'd had time to engage her thinking parts.

The phone rang. She and Everett had exchanged numbers, so she knew it could be him. *What am I supposed to do now?* In her mind, he would always have the heart of a hero, but weren't champions sometimes terribly flawed? The phone kept ringing. Could it be Everett was capable of goodness as well as deception? Or had she overreacted? Just as she reached to pick up the phone, it stopped its beseeching noise. The Caller ID let her know Everett had indeed called.

Lark went to sit in a place where life's puzzles seemed to unravel. Her tire swing. Flying-freedom-on-a-rope her mom always called it. She pushed off and then pumped her legs to fly higher and higher. At least as high as one could go in a tire swing. But despite its limitations, laughter always came, no matter what mood she was in. How could one not feel lighter while swinging free? Surely there would be tire swings in heaven.

As she peered up, she noticed the light playing hide and seek among the branches. She stopped her swinging and held her hand up to the glimmer, pretending the topaz-colored leaves were jewels on her fingers.

Lark slowed her pace and breathed in deeply of the brisk, fresh air. The snow had nearly gone, but there were still patches of the icy remains hiding from the sun. Picasso was in a jolly mood. He munched on something in the grass and then paddled around in his small pond. A duck's life looked so easy. Why couldn't her life be so simple? *A good place to sleep and eat and someone to love you.* Oh, there was that word again. Love. It seemed to stir up either euphoria or anarchy.

Lark turned her swing in circles until the rope made a cracking noise and would go no tighter. She lifted her feet and spun in faster and faster circles until she felt dizzy. She couldn't help but look up at Everett's office window when she made one of her last passes. She stopped herself when she saw something in his office window. It read: PLEASE CALL ME NOW!

Okay. How funny. So why didn't Everett just come to her front door? It's not like he'd build up any kind of sweat hiking over those twenty feet. Of course, it would help if she were in the house to answer the front door. Phooey. This was crazy. She needed to do something. Or maybe take a nap or watch a few minutes of the home shopping channel. No, not that last one. It would make her feel too pathetic.

Just as she rose from the swing, warm strong hands closed over hers. Most women would probably shriek about then or ready themselves for a karate chop. But even though she hadn't known the feel of Everett's hands long, she knew. It was him.

Lark turned around and looked up into Everett's eyes. Kind. Absorbing. Anxious. Yes, and he *should* be a little anxious, she thought, as she came to her senses. "How did you get back here?" She felt a little spirited all of sudden.

Everett released her. "Well, I opened the latch on your gate and walked through."

Why did his matter-of-fact statement make her want to laugh? "You are on private property." She stepped out of her swing.

"Oh, is that right?" He grinned. "I suppose my lack of an invitation has something to do with the view from your office window a few minutes ago?"

Lark folded her arms. Then she realized how ridiculous she looked as a spurned woman, tapping her foot and huffing.

"Don't you ever wear a coat?" Everett whipped off his tweed jacket and placed it around her shoulders.

She waited for a plausible counter from him, although having him closer to her made her forget a bit of what she felt anxious to know. *Closer* was the trigger word. Like a mousetrap on her finger. Yes, indeed. He'd been much *closer* to someone else just minutes ago. And she had long, platinum blond hair. *Oh, how cliché.*

"Apparently, the incident at the party last night caused quite a disturbance in the company. I haven't been doing much today except answering the phone and talking to women who've been harassed by Sylvester in the past. They've even come by to get advice. To sue or not to sue. I told them they'd need to pray about it and then seek the counsel of an attorney."

"Is that what you were doing in your office a few minutes ago? Praying with that woman?" Lark asked with a slight edge to her voice.

Everett's eyes widened. "And did you not see the part where I physically moved her away from me?"

"Yes . . . I . . . did." Lark felt a tremor of guilt. Well, maybe the tremor was really a six-pointer on the Richter scale.

"Madeline and I went out for coffee a few months ago. I wanted her opinion on something at work. I thought she and I might be friends since I didn't have any. But it appears to have backfired on me. She wanted more. But I was always honest with her. And as far as today, she said she dropped by to discuss Sylvester's harassment at work, but her real agenda surfaced pretty quickly. I'm sorry you saw it happen. But I have nothing to hide from you."

Oh, dear. Lark saw the sincerity in his eyes. She wanted nothing more than to embrace him and start the falling in love process all over again. But the speeding locomotive had already left the station and all of the emotional jostling would be part of the ride. There was no going back now. "Look, I hope you'll understand me when I say . . . I think I'm feeling something here," Lark said. "I've never acted this way before. I've got some new . . . *sentiments* I'm dealing with when I'm around you." *Yeah,* senti-

ments *was a good and safe word.* "And I
—"

Everett took her in his arms and quieted
her with a kiss.

*Yes, that's a very good way to deal with my
new sentiments.* She sweetened the moment
by returning his kiss with enthusiasm as her
arms wrapped around him. When the fervor
between them both heightened, Everett
gently pulled away.

"Woman, you've got quite a kiss there."
He let out some air and raked his hair back
with his fingers.

Everett's hair suddenly stuck up a bit,
looking kind of spiky. It looked so cute, in
fact, she wanted to muss it up some more.

"I think we'd better cool off for a second."
Indeed he appeared to have broken out in a
perspiring glow.

They both grinned at each other.

The air seemed filled with sounds again.
A car honked. A jet flew overhead. Funny,
how during the act of kissing, one became
insulated from the world. "Do you need
your coat back?" Lark asked.

Everett laughed. "Are you kidding?"

Was he actually trying to catch his breath?
Being thirty-five years old, surely he'd
kissed a woman before. Or maybe Everett
felt some new *sentiments,* too. "Why didn't

you have any friends?" Lark asked.

"There are a couple of reasons." Everett looked down at his loafers. "But when you're a slave to your job, it's one of the hazards."

Lark wondered what the other reason was for not having friends. He didn't say.

Everett lifted her chin to look at him. "Please go out with me tomorrow night."

"Will you feed me?"

Everett grinned. "Yes."

"Then I accept."

He felt the velvet strap on her overalls. "Everything you wear is so soft. Do you plan that every morning to be so appealing, or does it just come naturally?"

Lark gave him a one-shouldered shrug. She picked up an acorn and set it in his open palm. "Tell me, what do you see?"

To her surprise Everett held the acorn up between two fingers and studied it. "Well, from an accountant's perspective, I see potential . . . for growth."

"Potential is good," Lark whispered.

Everett put the acorn in his pocket and then lifted her hand to point to the tree above them. "And what do you see up there?"

"This big, old oak?" Lark thought for a moment as she gazed up into the branches and falling leaves. "I see a filter of light. A marker of time. And for birds, it's their birth, home, and first flight."

"Very perceptive. There's a painting in there somewhere." Everett released her hand. "But I suppose there is a scene to paint everywhere."

Lark suddenly wondered if he always planned to live in Eureka Springs. She knew her moving pains would be acute if she ever had to live anywhere else. "Don't you just love it here?"

Everett glanced over at his house across the fence. "Yes, I like my house."

"No . . . I mean Eureka Springs."

He smiled as if he knew what she was really asking. "You're here. So I wouldn't want to live anywhere else."

Lark breathed a sigh of relief.

Everett leaned over and gave Lark a slow, lingering kiss.

Okay, that felt very pleasant. She almost lost her footing.

"I'll pick you up at six . . . tomorrow evening." Everett squeezed her arm. "Casual. Okay?"

"I'll be ready," Lark said. Casual talk from a suit guy. Amazing. And he wore a green turtleneck instead of a button-down shirt. As he turned to leave, she remembered a question that had been tickling her curiosity. "Everett? May I ask what your middle name is?"

He looked back at her and groaned. "That information is given out on a need to know basis only."

"That bad?" Lark winced.

"Moss. It's Moss. You know —"

Lark tried to be polite and not chuckle. "You mean like the —"

"Yeah. Like the fuzzy, green stuff you tromp underfoot."

She laughed.

"But my mother liked it because Moss is a form of Moses, which means 'saved.' So maybe that redeems the name a bit."

"I believe it does." She found herself captivated by his golden brown eyes. Without thinking, she reached up to his face. Her hand was midway in the air when she heard Everett's cell phone come alive like a monster-sized beetle.

He frowned down at the phone, took it off his belt clip, and opened it to look at the screen. "It's somebody returning my call. I'm sorry, but I need to talk to him."

"Please, go. Take the call." Lark shooed him away sweetly. Everett mouthed the words, "I'll call you later." He answered the phone as he strode toward her gate. He'd forgotten his coat, but he didn't seem to even notice. She tugged it around herself, wanting to relive the warmth of his arms. She breathed in his scent. *Mmm. His cologne is spicy but sweet. Nice.*

As Everest closed the gate, she remembered his words about the woman in his office. "But I was always honest with her." How honorable. Had she been that straightforward with Jeremy? She hadn't led him on, but she really hadn't been clear about how she felt. This very evening, she vowed to make her feelings understood, even if it meant Jeremy would be disappointed. Lark had never liked confrontation, but if she expected to build a relationship with Everett then she would need to speak the truth to Jeremy.

When six thirty had come, Lark still hadn't quite figured out what she'd say to Jeremy. Skelly had been busy peeling and sautéing and baking in her kitchen to prepare his specialty — baked salmon with garlic mashed potatoes. *Sounds good.* Too bad she might not have much of an appetite.

Lark decided not to dress romantically for the evening since what she had to say might not seem too festive. She took one last glance at her suit and then headed into the kitchen. Delicious scents filled the house. She picked up a sprig of rosemary and took a sniff.

"You look nice," Skelly said. "Kind of like you're headed to a business meeting instead of a date, though."

Lark noticed Skelly's hairnet and forced herself not to chuckle. *Guess he was concerned about fallout. What had he said? Oh, yeah. I look businessy.* "Excuse me? And who said I shouldn't marry Jeremy?" Lark teased.

The doorbell rang. "Saved by the bell." Skelly busily retied his apron and adjusted his hairnet.

Lark sent up a quick prayer of supplication as she walked to the door and opened it.

"Hi. You look . . . nice." Jeremy raised an eyebrow.

"So do you." Once the compliment had come out of her mouth, she hoped it wasn't a lie. Jeremy wore a wildly-colored western shirt, so eye-popping in fact, it could replace caffeine. *Funny, I've never seen him dress that way before.*

Jeremy scratched his head. "You look very . . . professional. Like you're about to close some kind of deal."

She gulped the air. *What did he say?*

Maybe he could see the word *closure* in her eyes. "Thank you."

"Are you ready to go?" Jeremy asked. "I parked my bike off to the side of your garage door. That way you can back out your Hummer."

"Well, I've had a change of plans." Lark splayed her fingers in the air and faked a smile. *I must look like cartoon character.* "Our own Skelly from church is a gifted cook, and well, you know Skelly, don't you?"

The two men waved to each other from a distance. "Hey. How you doing?" Jeremy said.

"Good to see you," Skelly hollered back.

"And he's going to fix us our dinner," Jeremy said as if he'd come up with the idea.

"Do you mind?" Lark asked.

A pleased kind of smile crossed Jeremy's face. "It's a good move."

How could she not love this guy? So easy to please. But who knew the mysteries of love? One couldn't break the rules. *Even if I knew what they were.*

After Jeremy stepped inside, Lark took his leather jacket as Skelly strode over to shake his hand.

"Something sure smells good." Jeremy said. "Hey, you know we're in need of a cook at the church. We could sure use you.

There's even a small salary."

"Really?" Skelly fiddled with his apron. "But maybe you better see how you like my cooking before you offer me a job."

Skelly had set up the dining room table with candles, a white tablecloth, and her best china, but the candles were left noticeably unlit. Maybe he was trying to send her a subtle reminder.

Jeremy seated himself and then looked up at Lark. He chuckled and then rushed around to pull out Lark's chair for her. "My momma would beat me with a sharp stick if she saw what I just did. Sorry."

"No problem." Lark noticed Jeremy didn't smell like motor oil. *Much better.*

Skelly brought in the first course. *Vichyssoise.* After a prayer from Jeremy, Lark took a sip of the potato soup. *Yumm. Creamy. Thick. Satisfying.*

Jeremy slurped up a spoonful and then set the spoon down with a loud clank.

"Don't you like the soup?" Lark whispered.

Jeremy glanced behind him. "I don't want to hurt Skelly's feelings, but the soup is cold."

Okay, so what should she say? If she told Jeremy *vichyssoise* is normally served cold, it might hurt his feelings. If she sent the soup back for heating, it might upset Skelly. *Are there prayers for this, God, or am I on my own with this one?*

"Uh-oh. I've made kind of a booboo, haven't I?" Jeremy asked. "Is it supposed to be cold?"

Lark nodded and thanked God for giving Jeremy the heads-up, but she wondered why he was acting so peculiarly. He'd never been overly sophisticated, but he'd always been well-mannered. And he was missing that smirk she liked so much.

Jeremy gulped a few more spoonfuls and then squirmed in his chair. "Listen, before Skelly comes back in, I just have something I need to tell you." He tapped his spoon against his bowl as if he were doing a countdown before a launch of some kind. Then he stopped and looked at her. "I think you are one of the sweetest gals God ever made. Purdy as all get out."

When did he start saying hick words like purdy? Lark looked at him, thinking the real Jeremy must have been sucked up by aliens.

"And talented. And nice," Jeremy went on to say. "And kind. And purdy. Oh, I think I already said —"

"Jeremy, are you trying to tell me something?" *Oh, wow. I never saw it coming. Jeremy just wants to be friends, too. And here*

I thought I had the corner on miscommunications.

Jeremy took in so many short, fast breaths she thought he might hyperventilate. He fiddled with his napkin but looked at her intently. "I think we . . . you and I are best suited as —"

Skelly slipped in looking sheepish as he served the plates of baked salmon, sautéed veggies, and garlic mashed potatoes.

Jeremy's soliloquy halted.

Was Skelly coming in to eavesdrop? "This looks so good. I can't believe what you're *doing.*" Lark gave Skelly the evil eye and then grinned. *Boy, Skelly certainly got jaunty all of a sudden. Like a buoy in a gale.*

"Thank you. I hope it all goes down well for you." Skelly's hangdog expression changed to an all-knowing smile. *"Bon appetit!"* Then he disappeared.

Lark offered the silver basket of hot rolls to Jeremy, praying he would continue his speech. *Was Skelly actually listening in around the corner?*

Jeremy reached for a roll and began eating it. With a huge hunk of bread tumbling in his mouth, and while breaking every rule of etiquette imaginable, Jeremy said, "I think, Lark, we should just be good —"

The doorbell rang, making Jeremy nearly

choke on his roll. Skelly must have been shocked, too, because he dropped a metal pan on the kitchen floor. Lark just groaned.

SIXTEEN

"I am so sorry," Lark said. "I can't believe this."

"Neither can I." Jeremy let out a puff of air from his cheeks.

"It'll just take a moment. Please go ahead and eat." Lark placed her napkin next to her plate. "Be right back." She trudged to the front door and looked in the peep hole. *Oh, dear. Everett. How could this be?* Her date with him wasn't until the next evening. *Wasn't it?* It had never crossed her mind Everett would happen over on this scene because she wasn't having a real date. She was busy tidying up her life. Wrapping up some loose ends so she could focus on Everett. She looked again. He wore casual attire and carried a big load of groceries with a loaf of French bread sticking out of his bag.

Lark made the executive decision to open the door and calmly explain everything.

When the bell rang again, she yanked open the door. "Everett." Did she say his name too brightly? "Weren't you going to pick me up tomorrow evening?"

"Yes," Everett said. "But I just got back from the grocery store, and I bought too much food. So I thought I'd try being spontaneous for once and surprise you by fixing you dinner."

"You did. You did surprise me." *Okay, I guess that settles it. The hounds of Murphy's Law have finally caught up with me. And to think I've been an optimist all these years. What a waste of time.*

"Well? I make a mean macaroni and cheese. And I thaw the best cheesecake you've ever tasted. Have you eaten already? Lark . . . you're looking a little pasty. Are you okay?"

Hello. My name is Desperation. Lark finally opened her mouth to introduce everyone, but from observing the sudden downcast look on Everett's face, he must have already seen Jeremy sitting at the dining room table.

Everett turned around with his load of groceries and walked back down the path. The look of dejection in his eyes was enough to slay the coldest heart.

Lark wanted to shout something like, "There is a reasonable explanation for this," but she knew the words would come off hollow and soap operalike. Especially since she'd just made wild accusations against him which were false. Everett wouldn't be listening to anyone right now anyway. He looked too upset. Lark just watched him go and prayed God would give her a chance to unjumble the new mess she'd just made. Well, if falling in love indeed contained euphoria and anarchy, somehow she could guess which vat she'd just been dropped into.

It sounded as if Skelly tried to start some music on her stereo because he'd accidentally hit the French language CD instead. The teacher said, "Good-bye," and then, *"Au revoir!" How apropos.*

Slowly Lark plodded back to the dining table as if she had bricks attached to her shoes. Then she sat down in her chair with a thump. Apparently Jeremy hadn't missed her too much. He was busy constructing a little Tower of Babel with his mashed potatoes.

"Please go ahead," Lark said. "Unless we have a tornado or some volcanic activity, I think you'll be able to finish your sentence now."

Jeremy chuckled.

Out of the blue, Spanish guitar music

wafted in through the dining room speakers. *Good. Music will soften the uncomfortable edges of the moment.*

"I know we've been dating on and off for a few weeks now," Jeremy said. "But I just felt I needed to tell you . . . I see us as good friends more than anything else. I'm so sorry."

Lark freed a lungful of air, hoping she didn't sound too obvious. "Thanks for saying it first. I was about to tell you the same thing, but it's hard."

"Boy, you got that right. Like chewing on glass." Jeremy looked so thankful he reached across the table and squeezed her hand.

Funny, how she felt very little when Jeremy touched her. No stirring wonder. No electrifying euphoria. Just a soothing kind of brotherly comfort. But she still had a question gnawing at her. "Do you mind if I ask why were you acting like a redneck Neanderthal earlier?"

Jeremy laughed and took a long sip of water. "I don't know. I got this crazy idea if I acted like a jerk, maybe I wouldn't hurt your feelings that way. You know, maybe you'd be glad to be rid of me. But it just made me feel like a fool. Guess I forgot the words, 'And the truth shall set you free.' It's what I always tell the teens when I counsel them on dating." He shook his head. "Lark, I'm embarrassed by what I did. It was —"

"I know you did it with the best of intentions," she said with an earnest smile. "And I will always be glad to be your friend, Jeremy."

"Good move, Lark. For making an idiot look good."

Lark sighed. She watched as Jeremy rolled up his sleeves and dove into his meal with startling gusto. While he dug deeply into his salmon, Lark leaned over for a peek in the kitchen. She saw Skelly doing a little celebration jig with her broom. *Amazing.* Well, at least all appeared well with two gentlemen in her life.

Lark was obviously still dating the biker. Everett slammed the front door, making the window glass rattle. The door had already been shut, but he had a sudden need to open it and slam it again. In fact, he'd done more door-slamming in the last week than he'd done in his entire life.

He appeared to have been right all those years. Spontaneity wasn't all it was cracked up to be. People caused pain. Numbers didn't. What could be plainer or easier to grasp? He just needed to get back to the basics. Work. But even his job had taken a nosedive. How could his tightly woven way of life come unraveled so quickly? Everything had been going so well — a sterling example, in fact, of the good old American work ethic paying off. Until, of course, he'd moved next door to Larkspur. Now he'd lost his biggest client. *And a big chunk of my income.*

The reality of it hit him full force. Maybe the time had come to have a serious talk with God. So easy to give advice to other people about the power of prayer, but now when the going got tough, what was he really made of spiritually?

But perhaps all of the problems could have been avoided if Lark hadn't brought over my newspaper. Then Zeta wouldn't have invited her to the company Christmas party, which means Sylvester wouldn't have had the chance to be disgusting. But playing with the endless scenarios felt useless. Somebody had to stand up to the lout eventually. He just hoped God would reward him for doing the right thing.

But in spite of everything, Everett longed for the delight of Lark again. He shook his head. When had he ever needed *delight* before? He'd banned the word from his daily schedule years ago.

Delight. He opened a dictionary he kept

in a kitchen drawer and read the exact meaning. *Something that brings enjoyment. Hey, I can get enjoyment out of my combat simulation game and a double espresso.* And then he noticed the word *joy* listed next. He had to admit *that* emotion was harder to come by.

Everett slapped the dictionary shut and started putting his groceries away in the refrigerator. Milk. Juice. Bread. The essentials. But then he dug out other items from the bag he'd never purchased before. Caramel cheesecake. Vegetarian sushi. Maple-covered walnuts. All because he thought the items would please Lark.

But what nagged Everett the most was the guilty expression Lark had while he stood there with questions all over his face. And right after Lark had pelted him with queries of the same nature. She must be going out with a number of different men at the same time with equal earnestness. Or perhaps she was just dating that one youth minister with the rebel hair and kamikaze jacket. But his intellect told him to let go of Lark. *Now.*

Everett opened the freezer door and let the air cool his face. But who was he kidding? He wasn't about to let go of Lark that easily. Just because some beefy guy kept showing up with a ponytail and a macho

171

vehicle as if he'd just driven off the set of a "B" movie? He'd simply wait for the biker to exit, and then he'd fire a few questions at Lark. Perhaps he could utilize some of the same queries she'd bombarded him with earlier.

Everett closed the freezer door and sat down at the kitchen table to look over his list of contacts. Concentration would be difficult if he checked his watch every five minutes, but what else could he do? After he'd heard the rumbling of the bike next door, he waited another half hour.

Hoping Lark was finally alone, Everett changed into a green shirt and khakis and stomped over to her front door. As he reached up, the door magically opened. She stood there smiling at him guilt free. "I thought you'd never come."

"Well, I'm not coming in until I've had my say." He had practiced his spiel, and he felt determined to get it out.

"Okay," Lark said.

"I don't know the rules of dating very well, but I'm just going to say it straight out." He took in a little extra oxygen for support. "Yesterday evening felt unique. Memorable. I'm not talking about what happened with Ozark Consulting. I'm talking about us. Anyway, I'm not going to be dating anyone else. I thought you felt the same way. I'm hoping we can see where our . . . as you called them . . . our 'sentiments' are leading us. Do we have an understanding here? Are we clear?" Everett wondered if his words were coming off too robotic.

"Yes, sir. We're clear, captain, sir." She saluted and tugged on his coat, laughing.

Guess that answered my question. Everett frowned.

"Now will you please come in out of the cold?" Lark asked. "I promise what I have to say will make all things well between us."

"Is anybody here?" Everett looked over her shoulder. He couldn't believe in a matter of a few days he had gotten so possessive.

"No. Jeremy left about half an hour ago, and my neighbor, Skelly, left about five minutes ago. Please come sit down."

Everett managed to settle himself in the cushy, lavender sofa. Froufrou pillows surrounded him threatening to cut off his circulation, so he removed a few. Then he stretched out both his arms across the back of the sofa. He stared at Lark, waiting for her story.

Lark sat on the love seat across from him. "Jeremy and I have been dating on and off

173

for some weeks now. Mostly just going out as friends." She licked her lips. "Everyone in the church thought we would get married. They said we were a matching set. But I'm not totally sure what they meant." She fluffed one of the pillows.

Everett thought Lark appeared uneasy. He noticed she would either lick her lips or massage her earlobe when she felt uncomfortable. But he really wasn't in the mood to deviate from the subject. *Cut to the chase, Lark.* "And were the people in the church right?"

"No, they weren't." She fidgeted in her seat. "Since a certain man moved next door to me, I discovered I didn't want a matching set. Maybe in dishes, but not in marriage."

Everett rested his elbows on his knees. "And if I hadn't moved here, would you have married him?" He wasn't sure he really wanted to hear the answer.

"I think of him more as a friend. And besides, this evening, just as I was about to tell Jeremy how I felt, he said it first."

"You mean he dumped *you?*" Everett leaned back.

Lark furrowed her brows. "Well, I don't really think of it that way. I've gained a friend."

Everett laughed then realized how rude it seemed. "I'm sorry, Lark. I'm laughing from relief. I just spent some unpleasant hours next door concerned you were enjoying yourself too much over here. Well, you know what I mean."

Lark sighed. "I do . . . know what you mean."

"I don't know how to say the things I feel. I'm not even sure *what* I feel. It's as though I've known you for a long time."

"I feel the same, Mr. Holden," Lark said. "Kind of makes me want to sit next to you with some cocoa and a cozy fire."

Everett patted the cushion. "I think that can be arranged on this big, purple couch."

Lark got a match and lit some cinnamon candles on the coffee table. "Actually, the couch is lavender with violet flowers." She winked at him and headed into the kitchen.

He followed her and then watched as she brought out some cocoa packets from her pantry. "Need help?"

"Why don't you pick out some mugs up there." Lark pointed to one of the cabinet doors. "All I have is the instant kind of cocoa. Do you mind?"

"My untrained taste buds wouldn't know the difference." Everett picked out two mugs. One had a Michelangelo painting on it and the other had comic book characters. *Funny combo.*

She grinned at his selection of mugs as she poured in the whole milk.

"I like your casual clothes," Lark said. "You look nice in green."

"Thanks. And I've never seen you in a suit before. It's a great look, but then I'm beginning to think everything is a great look on you."

"Even a soiled evening gown?"

Everett nodded. "Even that." He leaned against the counter. "So is lavender your favorite color?"

"Yes." Lark popped the mugs into the microwave. "Lavender represents a coolness and a warmth at the same time. A calming pleasure to the eyes and a warming to the heart. At least it's how *I* feel about the color."

Everett had never thought much about colors. But when he wasn't wearing a suit, he tended to buy green shirts. Now he suddenly wondered why. Maybe it was because his middle name was Moss. "I want to remember what you said. It's important."

"Why?" She poured the cocoa packets into the hot milk.

Everett's hand covered hers as she stirred the cocoa. "Because you make me believe in life again," he whispered in her ear.

Lark looked a bit loopy all of a sudden.

"*And* you're the only person who's ever been able to knock me off the pedestal I put myself on."

She pulled back in surprise. "I didn't expect you to say that."

"Another danger of being a workaholic. In fact, my life had become a monotone, one-dimensional, black-and-white kind of existence. I don't really want to live that way anymore."

Lark reached up to touch his face. "I'm glad."

He touched her hand. *Lark is all of the wonderful opposites of my life. She's the depth, the variety, and the color I didn't even know I needed.* But he did. *Such romantic thoughts from a bean counter.*

When the cocoa had been heaped with marshmallows, Everett turned on the gas fireplace while Lark flipped on a Bach CD. They sat on the couch together, sipping on their beverages.

Harp music swirled around them. His arm settled around her easily as she nuzzled her head in the curve of his arm. It was as if they'd cuddled that way for years. Scented with roses, she felt soft and warm. *So this is what marriage will be like.* Suddenly the computer-espresso life appeared unfulfilling and trivial in comparison.

Lark set her mug on the coffee table. "I love the feel of your crisp, starched shirt. I'd love to have one of those."

Now who could have guessed those words would come out of her mouth next? Then Lark gave him a heavy-lidded look. It felt like the right time for a really great kiss, but he needed to know one more thing. "Lark?" He set his mug down.

"Hmm?"

"What is it you like so much about a starched guy like me?"

She grinned. "You do have a reticence about you — that's true — but there's also such a sweetness just under the surface," Lark said. "Even in this short time together, I can tell. You are like my favorite dessert."

"And what is your favorite dessert?" Everett asked.

"S'mores. You see, you have this crusty graham cracker on the outside, but inside I can tell there is all this sugary, creamy, marshmallow-and-chocolate middle oozing out all over the place."

"Oh, really," Everett said, enthralled by her amusing depiction.

Lark pulled out a lavender rose from a bouquet sitting on the coffee table. Her big, brown eyes looked up into his. "And I know right here," she placed her hand on her heart, "something special is happening between us. And I want to keep my heart open. I don't want to miss God's blessing."

Everett kissed the tip of her nose. No one had ever called him a blessing before. He didn't feel worthy of such high praise, but he liked the way she said it.

She lifted the rose to his cheek.

He took a whiff. *No scent.*

"You were trying to find the fragrance. These roses don't have any. But they bring pleasures in other ways."

"Oh?" Everett asked.

She stroked the petals along his cheek. "They are a piece of His creation and bring us beauty and wonder."

"Just like you." Everett couldn't imagine anything more wonderful than the woman who sat next to him. His words must have been appreciated, because Lark smiled at him, looking sweeter than s'mores. Everett gently swept her long brown locks over her shoulders so he could see all of her lovely face. Then he lowered his head to kiss her. *What a sensation! Floating again.* He'd kissed women before, but mostly to thank them for a nice evening. His contact with Lark fell into a category all by itself. He felt ready to tell her more of the things in his heart when suddenly his cell phone came to life.

Lark looked down at the buzzing interruption but didn't seem upset.

He glanced at the screen. The call appeared to be from Chet Riley, someone he knew at Ozark Consulting. "Maybe I'd better get this. I'm sorry."

Lark nodded, so he stood to take the call.

"Everett here." He mostly listened as Chet gave him the latest news. "Sounds great." Astonished and relieved with the promise of employment, Everett thanked Chet and said good-bye.

"What is it?" Lark asked. "You look dazed."

"I guess I am." He sat down. "Apparently, there's been an unexpected event. Sylvester is finally selling the company to Chet Riley. He's a good Christian man. I've known Chet a long time, and he wants me to replace Zeta as soon as the ink dries."

Lark threw her arms around him and kissed him. "Thank God. I've been praying for you."

"I prayed for a job, too, but I had no idea how it would work out." Everett shook his head. "I'm not sure why Sylvester sold out just now. Maybe it was the threat of reprisal from all the women he'd harassed. But I'm really glad he's gone. And everyone has you to thank for that."

"No. *You* were their hero last night. And mine, too." Lark snuggled her hand under his, and he squeezed it.

After a couple more tender kisses, they both promised each other to celebrate the next day. Since the weatherman guaranteed sun, Lark suggested an edgier form of entertainment — hiking at Beaver Lake. Everett surprised himself by agreeing. Since he'd never been a big outdoorsy guy, he just hoped he'd live to tell about it.

The following day, after hours of jam-packed spontaneous adventure, Everett not only survived the hiking, he thought he could take on just about anything. *Canoeing. Mountain biking. Motorized paragliding. Well, maybe not that last one. But the day has proven to be quite illuminating. And fun. Such a foreign word before Lark.* Even though he'd nearly tumbled down the side of a ravine once or twice, he felt a satisfaction that exceeded any previously known pleasures. In other words, he experienced joy with Lark. So simple and real, he couldn't stop himself from wanting more.

What a day! Everett tossed his keys on the counter and put away his coat as well as his brand new roller-blades in the hall closet. He smiled at the framed photo of Lark he'd asked her for. *Wouldn't do having her picture in the office. I wouldn't get a thing done staring at it, and besides, I have the real thing just a glance away.*

Everett set the picture on the coffee table and headed upstairs to his computer. It had been awhile since he connected with his other self. The feeling would be like going back to work after a long vacation, except usually he didn't take long vacations. He usually just worked. A lot. But now he felt rested and optimistic. Something that gave him a genuine smile.

As he sprang to the top step, the doorbell rang. *Couldn't be Lark. She's at a French cooking class. Maybe it's Chet.*

Everett trotted back down the stairs and opened the door. Someone with long hair, a beard, and shabby clothes stood on his porch. Someone who looked very familiar. His brain did a quick gathering of information. "Marty? Is that you?" Everett leaned closer to him. "What are you doing here?"

Marty held out his hands. "Coming to see my only brother."

Everett could barely get his mouth to move. "Where have you been all this time?"

"Doing a road trip to Hawaii." Marty

slapped his leg. "That's a little joke. Hey, aren't you glad to see me?"

Everett jerked his brain back to the present. "Sure."

Marty grabbed him with gusto. Everett lifted his hand for his usual pat but gave his brother a hug instead.

"Do I get an invite inside?"

"Sure." Everett opened the door and let him in. He went through the motions of leading Marty to the living room as well as adding a few pleasantries, but he really felt numb. Along with that bothersome tingly sensation. Everett tapped his face. The past came crashing back in a wave of grief. All that he'd kept at bay for three years. His elderly parents. The responsibility. The foolish decision. The accident. The funeral. "Why did you really come?" Everett heard himself say out loud.

Marty seemed to study him. "Hey, man, I haven't seen or talked to you since the funeral, so I thought it was time. You know."

"Yeah. You're right. It's been a long time. It is good to see you," Everett said. So much had passed between them, though, he just wasn't sure when he'd be ready to reunite the last of his family. But at least now he knew what had become of his brother. "Do you want something to eat?"

"I'm always hungry," Marty said. "Thanks."

"Okay." Everett noticed his brother still wore the same aftershave. The same one he always splashed on in his teen years. In fact, it had been their dad's favorite. "I've got some frozen entrees." Everett closed up his laptop on the coffee table and headed into the kitchen.

"Sounds good." Marty picked up the photo of Lark off the coffee table. "Wooow! Who's this?"

Everett didn't even need to glance back to figure out whom his brother was talking about. *Lark.* He wished Marty hadn't seen the photograph, but there was no time to hide it now. Maybe he could come up with a safe answer. "She's a woman I'm spending some time with." That sounded pretty lame when he knew he felt more than that.

"You're serious about her, aren't you? I know you wouldn't say that unless you had some serious feelings for her." Marty set the photo down.

How could Marty know me so well? They hadn't spent much time together since he'd left for college. He looked back at Marty. "Her name is Larkspur. And yes, I care about her." *Changing the subject would be good about now.* "So do you have a girl-

184

friend?"

A ripple of pain crossed Marty's face. "I did have a girlfriend, but she's gone now. Left me for a rich guy."

"I'm sorry. You've had a rough time these last few years since . . . well, you know."

"You can say it," Marty said without a hint of anger. "Since mom and dad and Greta died in the car accident. You're right. I haven't been doing so well. But I'm doing better now."

"And why is that?" Everett asked.

"Because I'm here with you, Ev."

Everett smiled, remembering a happier time when they were kids and Marty would always call him Ev. Seemed kind of strange to hear the nickname now. Haunting echoes of the past.

"Have you seen the house?" Marty asked.

For a moment, Everett wasn't sure what his brother meant. Then he realized Marty was referring to their old home in Fayetteville. He shook his head. "No. I haven't been back since — well, you know — since it sold." *Excellent time for another new topic.* "So where are you living now?" Everett asked.

Marty laughed. "That's the good part. I'm living with you now, Ev."

SEVENTEEN

Lark came in from her French cooking class with a monstrous appetite. All the foods she and her classmates had prepared were donated to a soup kitchen, so her stomach felt ready for some serious eating. She stood there with the fridge open. *Mmm.* "Let's see." *Whipped yogurt. No. Like eating flavored air. Grapefruit.* "Way too sour." *Ohh. Leftover quiche.* She reached down to the bottom shelf to pull out the pie dish. "Oh, yeah. Just right."

She wondered if Everett would be eating yet another one of his frozen entrees. He claimed they were gourmet, but how many of those things could a person eat? She imagined a block of frozen gravy slowly defrosting. Not a pretty sight. Maybe she could just slip over there and give him a slice of her quiche. He would love it. It was her best. Swiss cheese and crab. Before she could talk herself out of it, Lark covered the glass pie dish with plastic wrap. "Well, this is one night, Mr. Holden, you're not going to eat from a cardboard box."

Not bothering with a coat again, Lark ran up to Everett's house and tapped on his door. She hopped around trying to stay warm. A hairy sort of man who looked like Everett answered the door. *Who is this?*

"Woow. The gorgeous phantom from the photo. I'm Marty. Everett's younger brother. And you must be the woman he's falling in love with. Looks like my brother has very good taste."

Lark noticed Everett coming up right behind his brother. "That'll do, Marty." Everett playfully slapped him on the back.

Marty held out his hand to Lark, but she pulled him into a hug as she balanced the quiche with her other hand. "I'm so glad to meet you. I had no idea Everett had a brother. This is so wonderful."

"I can tell you're good for my brother." Marty opened the door wider. "And not just because you're a good cook." He winked. "Looks like you brought provisions. Real food."

Lark held up her offering. "I had some leftover quiche."

Marty took a whiff. "I don't smell anything, but you've got my stamp of approval."

"Thanks," Lark said. "I thought I'd bring it over since Everett always eats out of a box."

"Come on in," Marty said. "We can all break bread together."

Lark looked at Everett as she came inside. He smiled and escorted her into the kitchen, but Everett didn't appear happy about the situation. *How sad.* She would love to have had a sister or brother, but she'd been an only child. Perhaps a rift had come between them.

She glanced at them both again, intrigued with the comparison. Even though they looked a lot alike, their speech was poles apart as well as their clothes. Marty wore a dirty T-shirt and jeans while his brother looked as neat as a package of unopened napkins. She wondered if Marty had fallen on hard times or if he just lived a very laid-back lifestyle.

Everett heated up the quiche and found a bag of herbal greens while she and Marty brought out the dishes and flatware.

"How long do you get to stay?" Lark asked.

Marty chuckled. "Funny you should ask. I'd just told Ev I'd come here to live with him, but it was just a little joke. I'm passing through on my way to stay with a buddy who lives up in Missouri. But I love it here. These hills are full of poetry. You just have to be listening. That's all. Makes me want to pull out my guitar and cook up a song." He pretended to strum the prongs on the fork he held. "Composing and playing is like being airborne without a plane."

"I know just what you mean. I play the guitar, as well." Lark was amazed Everett had never mentioned any of it.

"Really?" Marty folded the last napkin and set the fork on it. "After we're finished eating maybe we could jam awhile."

Did a tiny groan come out of Everett? *Surely not.* Marty didn't seem to notice. She'd give Everett the benefit of the doubt. "Sounds good," Lark said. "I'd like that. I don't get to play with anyone very often."

"Is that what you do?" Marty asked. "Play professionally?"

"No. I illustrate children's books." Lark cut the quiche into slices. She couldn't help but notice that Marty had set the table as if he'd taken a home economics class.

Marty slipped his thumbs through his belt loops. "Just like my sister, Greta. She was an artist, too, before she died. Boy, she'd love everything about this town. The galleries, the music, the hills and woods."

"Sounds like you love it, too." Lark offered Marty a thoughtful smile. "I don't think I knew your sister was an artist."

"Yeah," Marty said. "She sure had a lot of promise."

Lark noticed Everett's expression seemed more like irritation than sorrow.

"So what book do you have out now?" Marty asked.

"My latest is *In a Giddy Pickle.*"

"Sounds cool," Marty said. "I'd love to see it sometime."

When they'd all sat down for the meal, Everett skipped the prayer, so Marty jumped in and said a quick one. Short, but with so much heart about his brother, the words brought mist to Lark's eyes.

Before Marty took a bite, he took the gum out of his mouth and set it on his plate. Everett looked at him but didn't say anything.

Marty shrugged. "Been trying to quit smoking."

"I've heard quitting is hard." Lark smiled at Marty. "Does chewing gum help?"

"Sometimes." Once Marty took a slice of the quiche and then a bite, he moaned. "All right. Now, Lark, this is a supremo quiche."

"Thanks."

"It *is* very good," Everett said.

Lark touched Everett's hand. "Thank you." Funny about the two brothers. They were indeed different, yet there were similarities as well. Their hazel eyes and build appeared identical, but sometimes they also had the same pensive look. People might read the expression as arrogant, but to her it appeared more like they were lost in thought at times.

"Are you coming back for Christmas?" Lark asked Marty.

"No," Marty said in a forlorn kind of way. "I don't think so." His eyes brightened as he made a drum roll on the table with his fingers. "Now I know who you are, Larkspur. *In a Giddy Pickle.* Yeah. I saw your book at the grocery store. They had this fancy stand for it. So how does it feel to be famous?"

Lark chuckled. "I've never thought of it that way. I love to paint, and kids seem to like what I do."

"The meek shall inherit the earth." Marty scrunched up his mouth. "Ev, if you don't propose to this woman, I will."

Lark looked back and forth at them, grinning. Everett stared at her with such a sad longing in his eyes she wanted to get right up and kiss it away. What could have made him suddenly so quiet and unhappy? Then she got an idea. Just a little one. Perhaps from God. Or maybe the idea really came from Sunday school when she was a girl. "I think we should play a game," she said.

Everett groaned again. Noticeably. "Sorry."

"Okay. I know it sounds corny, but what would it hurt?" Lark asked.

Marty turned to Everett. "You used to love games when we were kids. Greta and I used to call you the game meister. You were always the one we came to when we were bored spitless. Remember?"

"Yeah. I do," Everett said. "Okay. Let's try your game. What do we have to do?"

Lark took a sip of water. "Well, we each go in a circle a couple of times and just say something we like about the other person. I know —"

"Since there are no winners or losers, technically, it's not a game." Everett raised an eyebrow.

"We'll all be winners with this one, and it might be entertaining," Lark said.

Marty gestured with his hands. "Sure, why not?"

"All right," Everett said. "I'm not going to be made the Scrooge here, so let's go."

"Okay. I'll start." Lark folded her hands in

her lap and straightened in her chair. "I like the way Everett is firmly committed to things. Never wavering. And witty, even if he doesn't think so."

"Thank you," Everett said to Lark.

She looked back at him. "Your turn."

Everett held a forkful of salad in front of his mouth. "Okay. Marty's pretty decent on the guitar. Could have done it professionally, in fact."

"Thanks, man." Marty gave his brother a good-natured slug on the shoulder. "Never heard you say that before." He rested back in his chair. "Okay. Let's see. I like the way Lark sees things other people would totally miss."

Everett tilted his head at Marty. "You only met Lark thirty minutes ago. How could you possibly know something like that?"

"I don't know," Marty said. "Just a feeling."

Lark noticed Everett had a look of total confusion. Like he was in a dark room feeling around for the light switch. "Do you want to go another round? Or am I making you guys feel like you're in kindergarten?" Lark asked.

"It's kind of different," Marty said. "But it's not a bad kind of different. Okay, I'll start." He looked intently at his brother. "I like the way Ev sticks to things. He always reaches his goals. He's somebody any employer would want. All the right stuff."

Everett looked pleased. "Sounds like I'm hired."

Marty and Lark laughed.

Everett cleared his throat. "I like the way Lark smiles. She lights up the room. And she lights up people's lives." He opened his mouth to say more and then closed it.

"Thank you," Lark said. "Okay. My turn." She took in a deep breath. "I like the way Marty loves his brother. I would give anything for a brother or a sister."

"Well, if Ev marries you, you'll have me." Marty chuckled.

Everett stuffed a hunk of quiche in his mouth. He smiled at Marty, but it didn't seem like an expression of benevolence.

Oh, dear. "Could you really have played professionally, Marty?" Lark asked, hoping to soften the pressure on Everett.

"Yep." Marty rubbed his chin and stared across the room as if he were traveling back somewhere in time. "A group called the Living Legend. I tried out when they lost one of their guitar players. I made it in, but . . . I never got to play."

"I've heard of Living Legend," Lark said. "They play some good Christian rock. Do you mind if I ask what happened?"

Marty glanced at Everett, who had his lips in a hard line. "Bad stuff happened," Marty finally said. He waited for a moment and then went on. "Our parents and our sister, Greta, died. Car crash on some icy roads going toward Springfield, Missouri." He choked back some emotion. "I was the only survivor of the wreck."

"Everett mentioned the accident. I'm so sorry." Lark knew Everett didn't like to talk about the accident, so she let it go. She noticed the scar on Marty's cheek. Must have been from the crash. "So what do you do now, Marty?" Lark asked, hoping to diffuse the building tension between the brothers.

"I don't do much." Marty took a sip of his iced tea and then dropped in a few sugar cubes. "I kind of bum around mostly. Odd jobs. Friends help me out when I get in a bind." He took another sip and then added some more cubes. "Guess I'm kind of a drifter." He kept clinking his spoon around in his glass until Everett glared at him. He put his teaspoon down. "Seen a lot of this country but don't really have much to show for it."

"You *could* get a job. You could stay in one place," Everett said. "It's a choice."

Marty wiped his mouth on his napkin. "My choices sort of crashed along with the car that day of the accident." He wiped his mouth again.

"I'm sorry, but that's just a cop out." Everett threw down his napkin on the table.

Lark thought the two brothers might want her to leave. The moment felt more like a private family conversation. She sighed inside. The rift between them ran more deeply than she'd first imagined. "Should I go?"

No one responded. She felt invisible as they seemed transported back in time.

"It's not just about the accident, Ev. It's about you," Marty said.

Everett folded his arms. "How could it be about me?"

Marty paused as if weighing his words. "Because you never forgave me. You blame Greta and me for the accident," he said gently. "You always have."

"When did I ever say that to you?" Everett asked, raising his voice a notch.

"You didn't have to." Marty shook his head. "The blame was in your eyes. It was the day of the funeral. And it still is."

"Well, why did you take mom and dad out when you both knew the roads were icy? There was no emergency. You didn't have to take them clear to Missouri that day. You and Greta were always so reckless. Always had to push everything to the limit. Spontaneity was always paramount to responsibility." Everett rose.

Marty lowered his head. "We didn't know the roads were icy, Ev."

Everett straightened his shoulders. "But couldn't you have turned around when you saw the roads were getting dangerous?"

"The roads had been okay. But there was just that one bad patch." Marty touched his fingers to his forehead. "*One* spot. There's no way we could have known, Ev."

Everett dabbed at the perspiration on his face with his napkin. "But why did you always have to take mom and dad with you? Why?"

"Greta and I brought them along because we loved hanging out with them. And they loved coming along." Marty stood up and paced the floor. "Look, I've never mentioned this because I don't like putting you down, but somebody had to spend time with them and take them places. You didn't. You were always in a work mode."

"Working to pay off some of their hospital debts." Everett sat back down. "Somebody had to have a job. You and Greta were too busy living the artist's life to work a *real* job."

Everett glanced at her with regret in his eyes, but she still wanted to disappear. His last comment felt personal. Kind of stung her heart like a wasp with a double load of poison. Lark reminded herself that both brothers were wrestling with the past, finally bringing up long-suppressed emotions that needed to be addressed. She'd just gotten caught in a little crossfire, but she hoped it wouldn't injure their growing relationship. She placed her hand on Everett's shoulder, but he edged away. *Oh, God, please show me what to do.* Maybe it really was time to leave.

Everett traced his finger across his brow, looking drained.

"Please. I need to hear you say it," Marty said. "We can smooth so much rough road between us if you can just forgive me."

Everett looked at Marty and sighed. "If I say it, I want to mean it. And I'm just not ready. I'm sorry."

Lark bit her lip. *What an awkward silence.* Heart wrenching, in fact. When her parents had died in the crash, all the blame had gone to the drunk driver. Perhaps that fact had made the grief easier. Then she realized both Everett and Marty hadn't known such a strange comfort. They'd become paralyzed from a lack of closure. Each had reacted to the tragedy in a different, yet parallel way. Both had tried to escape into a hermit's life — one at home within the refuge of his computer and the other as a loner who couldn't attach himself to any one place.

Marty grabbed his coat off the back of the chair. "Listen. I've got some stuff to do. I won't be spending the night. I'll drop by tomorrow morning to say good-bye. Then I'll be off to Missouri." He looked at Lark. "Sorry about all this. Pretty heavy stuff. But I was glad to meet you, Lark." He reached over to shake her hand. "And I hope you won't hold this against us. Everett is a good guy. We just have some issues to work out."

Lark shook his hand. "It's okay. And I was glad to meet you, too, Marty. I hope someday we can play some music together."

"Me, too. Thanks." He shot Everett and Lark the peace sign. "See ya."

Everett started to rise, but Marty held up his hand. "I'll let myself out."

"Do you want to take the quiche with you?" Lark asked.

"No." Marty shook his head. "Thanks. Lost my appetite."

Lark felt a bout of righteous indignation coming on. Or maybe just pure fear that

Everett was entering dangerous ground. That he was closing off all those he loved just as her professor had years before. She gave Everett a look of disapproval with an imploring kind of smile attached as if to say, "Stop your brother and forgive him."

Everett seemed to ignore her pleading gaze, took out his wallet, and handed his brother a one-hundred dollar bill.

Marty just set the money back down on the table. "I didn't come for that, Ev."

"I know." Everett put the bill back in his wallet. "You don't really have to go."

"I don't think you understand." With those last words, Marty ambled to the door and left into the cold night.

If Lark thought the silence felt disheartening before, once Marty shut the door, a cheerless kind of gloom settled in around them in spite of the love she tried to offer him. There was *that* word again, but she couldn't turn back. Even if Everett shunned her now, she knew where she stood. Love could be a one-sided choice if it had to be, because no one could stop a person from feeling it. But caring for Everett made it even harder to watch him self-destruct from a lack of forgiveness. He'd been so hurtful to his brother and so irrational, she wanted to shake him. What could she say?

"I'm sorry you had to witness our dirty laundry," Everett said. "You can understand now why I didn't want to talk about it the other night."

Lark looked at him, wanting so badly to help him.

"Look, I know what you're thinking, and I don't need to talk this through." Everett shoved his food aside. "You're bursting to say something. Please, go ahead."

"I've gone through this," she said. "Not quite the same, as you know, but similar circumstances. I was forced to forgive someone."

Lark looked at Everett; his eyes were full of pain. She waited for him to speak, but he just gripped the table as if he couldn't let go.

"I didn't have to blame myself or any of my relatives for my parents' accident. That was the easy part." Lark moved her plate away. She'd lost her appetite, as well. "But I allowed the offender to write me from prison. He asked for forgiveness. I didn't want to do it. I fought it for about six months. And then I couldn't stand it any longer. Every single day I chose not to forgive him, I hurt inside. It kept extending the grieving period as it ate away at my spirit. So I asked God to help me."

"And He did it?" Everett asked. "Just like that?"

Lark shook her head. "No. I had to do it over and over until I really meant it, but God seemed to honor even my simple efforts to do the right thing."

"The right thing," Everett repeated. "You don't know the whole story. My brother and sister had a pattern of this behavior." He folded his arms. "My sister Greta was an artist like you, but she had a penchant for all things outlandish. And sometimes her tastes leaned toward the reckless. She took my parents hiking down in west Texas, and my father nearly died of heat exhaustion. I warned her, but she refused to take advice from her older brother. She was determined to do things her way even if it could hurt someone."

Everett stared off toward the front door. "My brother and sister were always alike. So wild and passionate about everything. They couldn't just *smell* the air before a rain. They had to go up in a plane during a thunderstorm and experience the source of the rain. So Greta could paint the rain with more realism and Marty could compose words about storms with more passion. How exasperatingly maniacal." He let his balled-up hand fall on the table, making a loud thud. "It's like I knew it would all end this way somehow, but no one would listen. No one. Now is that easy to forgive and flippantly dismiss?"

Lark looked at him intently. "Just because a person forgives someone doesn't mean it's done easily or flippantly. It's an act of courage." She paused and then felt an urge to continue. "And . . . the icy road Marty talked about. It sounds like he and Greta just didn't know. I mean, was the accident really their fault?"

Everett shook his head. "I'm sure you're trying to help me, but I'm just going to have to work this one out alone." He rose in his chair.

Lark took the cue and started cleaning up.

He took her hand. "No. I don't want you to do that. I'll get it."

Somehow his look pierced her heart. Everett was closing her out. She could sense it in every word and action. "Okay." Lark looked up into his handsome but sad eyes. "Is everything okay . . . you know . . . between us?" Her hands shook as she reached over to finger his collar. "I mean, I know I'm kind of spontaneous. And, well, artsy. But I hope you'll see it in your heart to —" She couldn't go on with her appeal since she felt close to tears. Lark licked her lips and fought to keep her chin from trembling.

Everett touched her hair. "I just need some time to work through this."

Is that true? Or are you trying to say goodbye? Lark put her hand over her mouth to steady her emotions. "Okay."

He kissed her cheek. "Why don't you pray for me? I'm sure I can use it."

"I will." As he walked her to the door, Lark looked around. She hadn't paid much attention before, but his house looked so empty. "You know, we haven't known each other long," Lark said. "But, well, I know this is putting my feelings sort of out there. But I think I'm —"

Everett gently placed his finger over her lips. "Are you sure you want to say this?"

Lark nodded. "I'm sure, even though I guess what I'm about to say will come off too impulsive, but it's what I want to say, so I'm just going to say it."

"I wish you would." Everett almost smiled.

"I think I'm falling . . . you know . . . sort of in love with you," she said. "Can't help it. It just happened, so I wanted to mention it to you." Lark could feel her words coming faster and faster like stones tumbling down a steep hill. *Oh, what a silly goose I've become.* "So, while you're working things through over here, at least you'll know how I feel over there." Lark kissed her forefinger and then touched it to his cheek. She hurried back to her house, not wanting Everett to see the tears that were beginning to flow.

EIGHTEEN

I'm a mess. I'm an absolute mess. Calli wouldn't even recognize me. Lark shut the door behind her and leaned against it for support. Even as a girl, she'd never been one for bouts of tears like some of her friends. With her sunny temperament, she'd always discovered lots of things to be fascinated with rather than moping for hours. But this wasn't a breakup from a schoolgirl crush. This felt like some serious peril to her heart. Or had Everett meant what he said? That he just needed some time.

Maybe I shouldn't have told Everett how I felt. But couldn't he see it in her eyes anyway? A dull ache trickled through her. *Not good. Okay, options. Paint, play guitar, Mocha Madness, pray, or call Calli. Or I could sip some Earl Grey tea and think of the needs of someone else.* Those were all good things, but first maybe she'd just treat herself to another round of tears.

Then she remembered what Calli had said — that God might have planted Everett next door for a reason. But what if the real purpose was to help Everett in some other way? What if the falling-in-love part wasn't destiny? *Wait a minute. Do I believe in destiny?* She groaned, wondering how her mother would respond. Maybe she'd say, "You know, honey, maybe you can't see the whole picture. Maybe God is working things out, and you just can't see it."

Okay, time for some prayer. Lark slipped on her gray sweats and knelt by her bed like she did when she was a girl. She surrounded herself with boxes of tissues like a fortress and began, "Please help me."

"Please help me," Igor repeated in his cage.

Lark slumped onto the bed. "Can't pray in *my* bedroom."

"My bedroom," Igor squawked.

Yes, I guess it is your bedroom. She smiled and shook her head at Igor. She decided to pray silently, and this time, mean it. *Please show me the way, and if Everett is meant only to be my good friend, then give me the courage to face it.* Then she thought of the severed relationship between the two brothers and prayed for a miracle of forgiveness and healing. Her own lack of responsibility and impulsiveness came to mind, so she asked for maturity in all areas of her life. She stayed on her knees until a peace washed over her like a warm bubble bath. *Maybe talking to God has more to do with sincerity and trust than the perfect words.*

Lark picked up the bedroom phone. Now for a good talk with her best friend. Calli's phone rang a couple of times, and then she answered. "Hey, girl. I was just thinking about you for some reason. Sent up a prayer, too. What's going on?"

"My emotions have been jumbled like they've had a few rounds in a blender," Lark said. "But I'm better now."

"Somehow I know this has to do with that neighbor of yours. You're either going to have to move or marry him."

"You don't know how true that is." Lark related the latest as Calli made noises of astonishment. "But I've given it to God," she finally added.

"It's all you can do," Calli said. "But I still think Everett needs to be slapped upside the head for good measure."

They both laughed.

"Wait a minute," Lark said. "I hear a funny noise in Everett's backyard. Hold on." Lark ran up to the loft with the portable phone to have a look. "You will never believe this. You know how Skelly throws pots and pans sometimes?"

"Yeah."

"Well, Everett thought it was so goofy. But I can see him doing it. He's got his backyard lights on, and he's out in the cold heaving pots against his brick wall."

"Oowwee. He must be in a bad way about his brother," Calli said. "And, you know, maybe he's wrestling with his feelings for you, too. Anger and love mingle in the same stream sometimes. I'll pray for him. But I've gotta go, ladybug. My doorbell is buzzing, and I have a date with one of the finest Christian gentlemen in Arkansas. We're doing my favorite thing."

"Let's see. Japanese cuisine where this samurai guy whacks up your steak in mid-air?"

"You got it."

Lark chuckled. "You go for it, girl, and then tell me all the finer points later. Bye." She hung up. *Well, that wasn't as satisfying as I thought it would be.* Usually Calli had more time to talk, but then she had a life, too. Calli certainly couldn't be expected to be on call twenty-four/seven just to listen to all her latest romantic catastrophes.

She couldn't help but wonder when one of them married someday if their friendship would change significantly. She would certainly miss their closeness. Their sister-hood. But even so, she hoped Calli had the most beautiful evening of her life.

Lark sighed and then stared down at the man who held her heart. Everett. *How did it happen?* Yes, somehow while she was busy helping Mr. New Guy out of his shell, he'd become Mr. Lifetime. She'd been minding her own business when love simply took her by surprise. Well, that wasn't totally ac-curate. She had indeed meddled in his life, but the surprise part was true. He had left her breathless. *And isn't that what I've longed for?*

Lark just hoped Everett was down there having a few good thoughts about her. Unfortunately, he had another pan in his hand, ready for a launch. *What could he be thinking?*

Everett rose from his deck chair and threw a saucepan even harder than the first one. *What a little minx.* Ever since he'd moved next door to Larkspur, every component of his life had been negatively altered. None of the past miseries with Marty would have been dredged up had it not been for her childish game. He would have made the best of his time with his brother, and then

Marty would have been on his way to Missouri in the morning.

Everett shivered even though he'd put on a heavy coat. He felt for his Palm Pilot, but it wasn't in his pocket. He'd always kept his Palm with him wherever he went, but at the moment he couldn't even remember where he'd left it. *My life is getting seriously out of control.*

Why did Skelly throw pots anyway? Seemed more insane than helpful. And it would eventually loosen up the mortar on his brick wall. He noticed all the dead mums around him, grunted, and trudged back inside. He felt so many intense emotions it frightened him.

Everett's head reeled with a headache. Where was his bottle of medicine? *Mental note: Buy five-year supply of painkillers. Or just move away from Larkspur. Same effect.*

He couldn't find the medicine in any of the usual spots, so as a substitute, he sat in front of his computer. *Long time, no see, old friend.* It's great to be back in the pilot seat. He didn't bother looking over at Lark's office window. He refused to succumb to the temptation this time, and instead gazed into his real world. *Ah, yes.* The soft glow of the screen was like a reassuring friend. And he'd have a good, steady job soon. Maybe with some discipline he could make the rest of his life just as it had been.

Everett flipped on his stereo. *Liebestraum* by Franz Liszt was playing. *Hmm. Not very invigorating to get the juices flowing.* He changed CDs to Mozart's *Allegro. Now, that's a little more like it.*

But every time Everett stared at the screen for more than a minute, those big, brown, impish eyes of Lark's seemed to be staring back at him. Full of sweetness. Then he summoned up a more recent expression of hers. At dinner with Marty, her glow hadn't been so loving. In fact, her look at him had been reproving, or at the least, pleading.

He leaned back in his chair, making it moan. Even his chair seemed against him. Could Lark have been right? Had he been too tenacious with his views, and had his lack of forgiveness eaten away at his spirit? Granted, Marty and Greta had always relished proving they were covered with some kind of invincible powder, and he'd always been more than willing to take up the role of the nay-saying, older brother, but all of that aside, had the accident truly been their fault? One unforeseen patch of ice causing them to career into a ravine. *Maybe the same thing would have happened if I had been driving. But then how could it have happened with me? As Marty said, I never took Mom and Dad anywhere.* Had it been true? Had he been so busy trying to impress his parents with hard work that he'd forgotten to just be their son?

He flipped off his music. Oddly, he only listened to the classical music to stimulate his mind for higher productivity, not because he had a passion for it. He felt like a fraud.

Back to his headache and what felt like the beating of a bass drum inside his skull. Everett yanked open one of the top drawers on his desk, thinking he might have stuck his medicine inside. *No medicine. Great.* Instead he saw some crumpled documents inside. He rummaged through the pile. *Hmm. Old insurance paperwork. Funeral expenses for Mom, Dad, and Greta. The brake job on my last car.* Brakes. *Why does that word always stick in my head?* In fact, for the last several years, every time he heard that word, it was as if he were searching in his mind for a lost piece of a puzzle.

Brakes? My car. My family's funerals. Mom and Dad's car. My responsibility. That's right. Once his parents had gotten elderly, Greta and Marty had watched over their house, but it had been his job to take care of his parents' car. Had he forgotten about some car repairs? *Brakes!* That was it. He was supposed to have had their brakes worked on. Had he been too busy? Why had he blocked it from his memory . . . until now? Out of convenience? Hidden guilt?

Everett squeezed the temples of his forehead. He'd let his parents down, but more than that, perhaps the brakes were the real problem when the car went out of control. His body jolted back in the chair. A dead nerve seemed to twitch back to life. *What's happening to me? Maybe now I'm feeling the stinging guilt Marty has suffered for years.*

Everett took out a handkerchief from his back pocket and wiped his forehead. He put his hand to his stomach. All of a sudden he felt quite ill. He raced to the bathroom just in time to throw up in the toilet. Was it bad quiche? Maybe Lark was interfering with his stomach now. He already knew the answer as he leaned over for another heaving wave of nausea. *The food isn't the problem. It's your life.*

He allowed dozens of thoughts to drift in and out of his consciousness. His life had become just like his parents' car. Careering off into an abyss. He'd missed so much. A relationship with his brother. The volunteer work he'd given up. Friendships he'd walked away from. He flushed the commode and

214

wiped off his face.

And why had he insisted on closing up his heart all these years — the coldness masquerading as a good work ethic. To punish his brother? To destroy himself?

Or had he conjured up some magical thinking? He wondered if subconsciously he'd kept emotionally vacant in case that could keep life from zapping him again. And did his noxious mixture of emotions include anger toward God? So many questions.

Once his stomach settled, he knew what he had to do. Since he was already on his knees, he decided to stay there. *God, where do I even begin with this prayer? How can You forgive me for what I've done to Marty? I guess people don't have to be artsy to be irresponsible. Obsession with my career has accomplished that very well.*

Everett continued his prayer, asking for forgiveness and guidance. Then he rose feeling different. He knew the cold, dispassionate cement he'd built around his heart was crumbling down. *Okay. I guess I've got a job to do, and this time it won't be at my computer.* The relationship with his brother had suffered too long with a festering wound. The time had come for healing.

Just as he headed to the bathroom for a shower, the doorbell rang. *Lark? Marty?* He hurried to the door. When he opened it, he found a woman standing on the porch looking anxious.

"May I help you?" Everett asked.

"I'm your neighbor, Melba Sanders. Next door to Lark."

"I'm Everett Holden." He noticed the older lady had a pleasant smile and held a plant of some kind.

Melba reached out her hand to him. "Pleased to meet you."

Everett shook her hand. "Same here. Would you like to come in?"

"Oh no, thank you. I just brought over this little ivy plant here to welcome you. I wanted to bring it last week, but I had a run-in with my gout."

"I'm sorry to hear it." Everett accepted the houseplant, which sat in a small, wicker basket. "Thanks for the plant."

"Oh, you're welcome. I would have baked you a cake instead, but I'm a terrible cook," Melba said with a pleasant chuckle. "Yes, indeed. One of my floppy cakes is no way to meet and greet a new neighbor, I always say." She titled her head as she took in a deep breath. "But I also stopped by to tell you Sam Wentworth, next door to me, is in the hospital with a broken wrist. Sam should be fine in no time, but I just wanted you to know. We all keep up with each other around here."

Everett thought maybe he should help in some way. "Should I go and see Sam . . . in the hospital?"

"Oh, no need to go right now. Lark is there. But it's nice of you to ask. You know, you're going to fit in really well here, Everett. Yes, indeed."

Once Melba had gone, her words still clung to him. *No need to go. Lark is there.* If there were ever a problem or a need, Lark would always be there because she was the kindest, most generous human being he'd ever known. Not to mention a woman with the sweetest kisses.

Now that Lark had gone to the hospital for a visit, the neighborhood did seem quiet. *Too quiet.* He missed her electric guitar adding her own wild additions to his classical music — two very distinct genres of music, yet they meshed in some strange and wonderful way. *Just like we do.*

Everett fell on his bed, exhausted from an overload of feelings. He gazed at the moonlike ceiling. He'd thought of himself as such a rock, but Lark had managed to tenderly smash his indomitable mind-set with her dainty, velvet mallet. One week in the shadow of those intense eyes and he was

217

toast. Worthless to do anything but love her.

The fact remained, Lark would always be an artist-type with a grin brimming with impetuosity — a real loose cannon with some zany added to the fuse. But Lark was also the dearest woman he'd ever met. *The only question that could possibly remain is — should I marry her?*

Everett drifted in and out of sleep all night. In the morning, he awakened sweaty and tangled in his bedding as if he were Scrooge waking up from a horrific night of time travel. As his dreams gained clarity in his mind, Everett realized he'd indeed been like Scrooge — stingy with his money *and* with his feelings.

In one of his nightmares, he'd seen his epitaph: *Here lies Everett Moss Holden III, a miserly bean counter, survived by no one.* He'd tried to run, but as in most night terrors, it became impossible to even move a muscle. He'd thought, *No. I don't want to grow old alone. I want to give more — love more. Well, at least all my nightmares finally have some good use.* He knew now his life needed some modifications.

Everett rose from his bed and sat down at the kitchen table to write out his apology to Marty. When he'd finished pouring out his thoughts onto the paper, he tore up the letter and decided to talk to his brother straight from the heart. He gazed into the living room at the piano. *Who knows? Maybe a dose of forgiveness and some music will ease my nightmares and headaches.*

He took a stroll to the coffee table to pick up Lark's photo. He smiled as his hand went to his heart. Everett vowed that after he made all things right with his brother, he would take care of some business next door, as well. Maybe he'd even utilize a little spontaneity again. "Okay, Larkspur Wendell, prepare to be dazzled."

NINETEEN

Lark woke up thinking about Everett, and she wondered how a creative God planned on working out all the messy details of their lives.

She smacked her lips. "Oww." Her mouth felt like a litter of dust bunnies had played all night in there. And had she aged ten years overnight? How in the world had she made it past age thirty without needing coffee in the morning? Suddenly she wanted some. *A large amount. Right now.*

After two large mugs of French roast and a visit to her tire swing, Lark made her way up to her studio loft. She was eager to squeeze some fresh oils onto her pallet and load her camel-hair brush with paint, but she knew the sketch on her canvas still lacked something she couldn't quite grasp. The balance still looked off, and there was no intrigue. No *joie de vivre*. But maybe God would give her the inspiration she needed today.

As she stared at her canvas, Lark detected a movement out of the corner of her eye. She looked down into her neighbor's backyard. Everett appeared to be putting up a birdfeeder. He dropped the huge thing on his toe and then hopped around in pain as seed spilled everywhere in his backyard. Lark gasped, wanting to help him. Everett patiently refilled the container, hung it up on the tree limb, and then sprinted back down the steep hill to his house. *Why is he running? What is he up to?*

Lark looked back at her work. Maybe she just needed some sugar reinforcement. *Jellybeans. Yes.* Lark glanced into her big glass bowl. *Empty!*

Okay. Calm. There was plenty of backup licorice in the desk drawer. She pulled out two sticks and let them hang out of her mouth as she chewed. Before long, she had both pieces consumed. *Mmm.* Creativity flowed more easily on a sugar high.

Did I hear the doorbell? Everett? Lark dropped her pencil in the jar and trotted down her spiral staircase to open the door.

"Skelly. How are you?" Lark tried not to show her disappointment.

He had a funny expression as he touched his lips. "Uhh. You've got — well, your lips and mouth area sort of look gray. Are you okay?"

Lark thought for a moment and laughed. "I've been on a licorice binge."

"Oh." Skelly grinned. "I don't have time to come in, but I had some news. Jeremy made me a formal offer to be the chef at the church. It's not a lot of money, but I think I would like it. What do you think?"

"Yes, it's perfect. What a God-gift." Lark hugged Skelly, noticing he'd put on some fresh clothes and he had a faint smile on his lips.

"And the Valentine's banquet is coming up, and I'd like you to play that song you entitled 'Rose,' " Skelly said. "Would you?"

"I'm a little rusty," Lark said. "Maybe you can sing harmony with me."

"You bet." A shadow passed over his face. "You know, I think my taking this job would please Rose. I thought maybe she'd be upset with me if I sort of just wasted away down here. Maybe she'd want me to do something more useful than just throwing pots and pans."

Lark smiled. "I think Rose would be very proud of you. Just as I am."

"You gave me the courage to do this. I guess what I really came over to say this morning was . . . thank you." Skelly wiped his eyes.

They hugged again, and then Skelly hurried down the stone walk but this time with purpose in his step. *What a difference a week can make.*

Skelly mentioned the word courage. In fact, that word had been popping up a lot lately. Lark glanced up and noticed the bracelet Calli had given her. It sat on the entry table as a reminder of her pledge. How odd to push Everett toward bravery, and yet she didn't have the guts to follow through with her promise to Calli. She slipped the delicate pearls on her wrist. Such lustrous beads from the stress and strain of humble creatures. Something so lovely coming from so much pain. Life was just that way sometimes. For Everett and for her and for everyone.

Well, she certainly couldn't force Everett to fall in love with her. She could only apologize for her rambunctious spirit, love him, and pray for him. In the meantime, she would follow the path the Lord had made clear. What had Calli said? "Your art is a gift from God, and He expects you to share it."

Lark nodded as she headed toward the kitchen. After all, how could she encourage others to follow their dreams when she kept hers at a safe distance? She wondered how she'd allowed such a large facet of her life to become so weak and cowardly. Was it from being an only child? Too pampered growing up? Or had she known too much success too soon, and now she secretly required all life-journeys to be easy?

Whatever the reason, the time had come. Lark pulled out the kitchen drawer that contained the small directory of galleries — a list she'd been avoiding for a long time. *Today, I will follow through with my future, even if it doesn't include Everett.*

Her last thought gave her some real heartache, but she knew she would keep her pledge no matter what happened. Lark blew out a puff of air. She reached for a backup package of licorice from the pantry and stuck two more twists in her mouth. *On the other hand,* she thought, *maybe when Everett put up the birdhouse, it was a sign of change.*

The doorbell rang again. *Everett?* This time a shy-looking stranger stood on her porch. He stuttered a bit and then handed her a huge bouquet of lavender roses. She thanked him with a tip and a hug. He looked at her funny, blushed profusely, and scuttled back to his van. Lark opened the card. It read, *I am a lone vase, and you are the bright flowers that fill it. Affectionately,*

Everett. *P.S. All is well between Marty and me now, thanks to God and a little neighbor lady I know.*

Guess it's my turn to cry. Lark kissed the card as she blinked away the tears. She looked up at the Almighty and thanked him for helping Everett. If he had ever been on the same road as her old professor, Dr. Norton, he certainly wasn't now.

Then Lark got an idea, but this time she knew it wouldn't muddle anyone's life, another step to being more responsible in all areas of her life. She finally realized what had been missing on the canvas in her studio. The young woman had been alone in her garden. She'd been content and had even donned a faint smile on her lips, but the path to the garden had also been empty. If Lark sketched in a gardener coming up the path toward the young woman with his hands full of lavender roses, people would be moved. Well, at least Lark knew she would be stirred by the scene. *Yes. Two people, poles apart, coming together for a lifetime. Loving each other even when everything seemed against them.*

Lark put the roses in a vase and trotted up the stairs to her loft. Once she'd sketched in the gardener, it would complete her vision for the painting. And she prayed it would be her finest.

Just as she reached for her pencil, the doorbell rang again. This time about ten times in a row. *I'm coming. I'm coming. Couldn't be Everett. He would never ride the doorbell like that.* A deliveryman the size of a grizzly bear, spewing some pretty creative adjectives, handed her a big box with a lavender bow.

She accepted the gift and handed the man a tip, but he continued to stand there as if he were waiting for something else. Surely he didn't want to know what was in the box. *Isn't this supposed to be a private moment?* Oh well. Maybe he was friendless and never got any presents. So Lark decided to rip open the box in front of him. She never could open boxes with dignity and patience. In fact, she felt like some squealing was in order when she tore back the tissue paper and gazed at the gift inside — a starched, white shirt all folded up neatly. She pulled the shirt out of the box and laughed. *Everett actually remembered what I said.*

"Must be a private joke of some kind," the man said.

"Yeah. It is." She pulled out the card and read it out loud. "I was never good at giving gifts to women. Until now. You inspire me! Yours, Everett."

The big guy nodded. "That's real nice."

Did he actually sniffle?

"Well, have a good day," the man said, giving her the same strange look as the other delivery guy. He lumbered off the porch and back into his flow of delivering objects of importance from one life to another. Lark recognized his lonesomeness and breathed a prayer for him.

Immediately on shutting the door, Lark put the shirt on over her sweats. *Nice. Crisp and fresh.* Then she reminded herself not to paint in it.

The doorbell rang again. *Boy, maybe I should just prop the door open with my shoe.*

This time the delivery guy was a teenaged girl from one of the local grocery stores. "Hi. Are you a" — she stopped to look at the clipboard — "a Larkspur Camellia Wendell?"

"That's me."

"This is for you then." The girl handed her the box. "We don't usually do deliveries, but I offered to come. I already know what it is. I made up the box a few minutes ago."

The young woman looked desperate to tell her what she knew. "Okay," Lark said. "So what's inside the box?"

"S'mores. Can you believe it?" The young

woman went at her gum like a cow chewing in fast motion. "I mean, guys used to call the flower shops and have flowers delivered, you know what I mean? Now they call the grocer for cheap candy, marshmallows, and graham crackers. I mean, hello? How cheapo is that?"

"I think it's perfect." Lark handed the teenager a tip.

The young woman motioned to her mouth. "Well, I sure hope you love this guy is all I have to say." The girl's grin showed almost all her teeth. She walked off, still chatting. "Men. It's like they don't get it. They're from Pluto. Or is it Mars?"

Okay, that was a semi-weird encounter. In spite of the cold weather, Lark left the door open this time. Just in case Everett showed up as her next surprise. She opened the box with one tearing sweep. Sure enough, inside the box were all the makings for s'mores as well as a few packages of cocoa. She read the card that came along with the gourmet s'mores. *Please invite me to your church. I'll bet you'll get a different answer this time.* He'd signed it, *Love, Everett.*

Lark did a little jig. Guess she had a few things to share with Calli. But when Lark pulled the goodies out of the box, two folders fell out. She opened them. *Oh my, my, my. Two airline tickets to Paris? I can't believe it. No wonder the delivery girl was grinning from ear to ear when she walked away.*

At that thought, the man of her dreams, who also happened to be the boy next door, came striding up the walk wearing a tux. When Everett arrived at the front door, he wrapped his arms around her and kissed her before she could even let out a single thank you. And among kisses, it had to be a ten. What Lark would really call a crying-in-your-popcorn, chick-flick kind of kiss, intended to make all the females in the audience cry a river. "You are so *my* guy. I guess this means you forgave me for all my impetuous meddling. My silly games."

Everett pulled away for a moment. "Well, what happened with my brother was long overdue."

"But I am sorry."

"You are forgiven." Everett picked her up and kissed her. "By the way, did I get it right? The romantic thing?" he asked with a bashful grin.

"Oh, you got it *very* right."

Everett tugged on the tail of her starched shirt. "I like your shirt."

"Me, too." Lark cocked her head at him. "Hey, you must have been taking a crash course in romance lessons."

"Not really. I think it was all there. Just didn't want to waste it on all the wrong women." Everett grinned.

"But Paris?" Lark shook her head. *"Tres bon!"*

"Well, since you're learning the language and all." He shrugged and grinned.

Mist stung Lark's eyes. "I've never been to Paris before, but I've always wanted to go." She let out a big breath of air.

"And of course, there is the Louvre in Paris," Everett said. "I thought you might have a bit of interest there."

"Interest? The paintings! The sculpture!" Lark bit her lower lip. "I've dreamed of going there ever since I was a little girl. I suppose that's why I've been learning the language. But I'm not sure why I've never gone."

Everett pulled her to him. "Because you were waiting to see it all with me."

"Yes. I suppose that's it, and I just never knew it, until now. I can't think of anyone I'd rather share Leonardo's *Mona Lisa* with than you." Lark absorbed all the love of the moment. In fact, she felt certain this very scene would wind up in a painting someday. "Thank you so much." Lark kissed him again, just to make sure the moment was real. "By the way, you look very fine in your tux. Are you wearing it for any particular reason?"

"I wanted to ask you out tonight . . . only I wanted to do it in style since I'm taking you to the Whitestone Bistro on Beaver Lake."

"Really?" Everyone in the area knew Whitestone was *the* restaurant for serious romance.

Everett looked down at her lips and grinned. "Your lips are extra sweet, but they are the color of my tux."

Color of his tux? His tux was gray. Lark pulled back in horror. She glanced in the mirror. She'd forgotten that her lips were tinged dark gray from eating licorice sticks. Lark laughed. "And you still *kissed* me? So that explains why the delivery people kept looking at me funny."

Everett threw his head back in laughter.

Lark liked the way he looked down into her eyes with such tender love. "I got your note about Marty."

Everett shared all the revelations of the night. Then Lark's heart soared with joy when he told her of his apologies to his brother and their reconciliation. "I'm so happy for you both." She squeezed his hand.

"Oh," Everett said. "And I discovered some essentials."

"And what are those?" Lark kissed him on the chin.

"Well, the important stuff can't be found in the hard drive of a computer, but right here." He lifted her hand up to his heart. "Do you want to know what else I see?"

Lark nodded. "Yes, I do."

"I see you and what you are to me," Everett said. "My *joie de vivre* . . . my sweetness of life."

Okay, now is that romantic or what? Lark swallowed a giggle.

Everett gently caressed her lips with another kiss.

She wiggled her eyebrows. "Oh, this is way better than a chick-flick."

Lark suddenly remembered the little acorn drama in her backyard when she'd first met Everett. She knew God would somehow allow their lives to bounce off each other, touch each other, and change each other. But whether acorns or humans, she knew the conclusion would always remain the same. Life was pure adventure.

EPILOGUE

Lark was pleased to discover that White-stone Bistro had all the romantic delights everyone had boasted of. She enjoyed many more evenings there with Everett as well as sunny afternoons hiking and heart-to-heart talks about their faith and their future as they strolled the downtown shops along with the tourists.

Then one morning Lark took another joyride on her tire swing. When she slowed to a stop, warm hands covered hers. She turned around to see Everett standing over her. He held a small, velvet box in his fingers.

Lark put her hand to her mouth. "Is that for me?"

"It is," Everett said. "Unless you think Picasso might like it more."

She laughed as she accepted the gift. *I can't believe this is finally happening to me. Let the earth know that on this glorious*

Arkansas day, Larkspur Wendell will say "yes" to Everett Holden. She slowly raised the lid. The hinges made a little crackling sound before the box snapped all the way open. Lark gasped. Sitting cozily in the black velvet rested the most eye-popping, marquee diamond ring she'd ever seen.

Tears welled up in Lark's eyes as she looked at the ring and then back at her Everett. "You leave me breathless."

He touched her cheek and wiped away the tear. "I hope that is a good thing."

"It is . . . a *very* good thing." Lark ran her fingers over his arm as she looked into his golden-brown eyes.

Everett knelt down on one knee in front of her. "I guess I've been waiting for you all my life, and here you were. Right here." He took in a breath and smiled. "Larkspur, will you be my one and only? I've never known anyone like —"

Lark hopped out of her swing and kissed Everett with fervor. She hadn't formally said yes, but Everett seemed pleased with her response. Even Picasso waddled around in his pen with more gusto.

Over the next few weeks, Lark and Everett planned a simple, but elegant wedding. The ceremony would take place in a chapel nestled on a hill not far from the famous

Christ of the Ozarks statue. They also chose the church for the magnificent scenes in the stained glass windows, which they hoped would remind all in attendance of the greatest love gift of all.

On the big day, Skelly proudly escorted Lark down the aisle to give her away. When Lark arrived at the altar, the pastor asked, "Who gives this woman in marriage?"

Skelly sniffed a bit. "I do."

Lark squeezed Skelly's trembling fingers as he lifted her hand toward the man she adored. She met Everett's gaze. He looked so handsome and loving she thought her heart might burst from joy. *Oh, Mom and Dad, I wish you were here.*

Later at the reception, Lark lifted her bouquet to an eager crowd of single women. She aimed the flowers at her dearest friend and maid of honor. Calli caught the flowers intended for her with one hand. Lark also pleasantly took note that several of the single ladies seemed to be clustered around Everett's brother and best man, Marty.

When the day's festivities had come to a close, Lark and Everett dashed through a rain of pelting rice and into a white, stretch limo waiting for them by the chapel. The next morning they caught an early flight to Paris. First class.

Their honeymoon in Paris was full of delights with leisurely walks down the *Champs Elysées,* visits to the Louvre, lunches at the local bistros, and the services provided by their hotel, including the sign Lark enjoyed hanging on the door that read, PLEASE DO NOT DISTURB.

ABOUT THE AUTHORS

Anita Higman hopes to give her audience a "gasp and a giggle" when they read her stories. She's the award-winning author of eighteen books. Anita has a B.A. in speech communication and is a member of American Christian Fiction Writers. Anita enjoys hiking with her family, visiting show caves, and cooking brunch for her friends. Please drop by her book café for a cyber visit at www.anitahigman.com.

Janice A. Thompson is a Christian author from Texas. She has four grown daughters and the whole family is active in ministry, particularly the arts. Janice is a writer by trade, but wears many other hats, as well. She previously taught drama and creative writing at a Christian school of the arts. She also directed a global drama mission's team. She currently heads up the elementary department at her church and enjoys public speaking. Janice is passionate about her faith and does all she can to share it with others, which is why she particularly loves writing inspirational novels. Through her stories, she hopes to lead others into a relationship with a loving God.

The employees of Thorndike Press hope you have enjoyed this Large Print book. All our Thorndike, Wheeler, and Kennebec Large Print titles are designed for easy reading, and all our books are made to last. Other Thorndike Press Large Print books are available at your library, through selected bookstores, or directly from us.

For information about titles, please call:
(800) 223-1244

or visit our Web site at:
http://gale.cengage.com/thorndike

To share your comments, please write:
Publisher
Thorndike Press
10 Water St., Suite 310
Waterville, ME 04901